DETOURS

TWELVE STORIES

CYNTHIA DENNIS

CKBooks

Publisher's Cataloging-In-Publication Data
Names: Dennis, Cynthia, author.
Title: Detours : twelve stories / Cynthia Dennis.
Description: New Glarus, WI : CKBooks Publishing, [2019]
Identifiers: ISBN 9781949085167 | ISBN 9781949085174 (ebook)
Subjects: LCSH: Compulsive behavior--Fiction. | Deviant behavior--Fiction. | LCGFT: Short stories.
Classification: LCC PS3604.E58633 D48 2019 (print) | LCC PS3604.E58633 (ebook) | DDC 813/.6--dc23
LCCN: 2019941112

Cover design: Simon Cellard ◆ Visual Designer
simoncellard4341@gmail.com

CKBooks Publishing
PO Box 214
New Glarus, WI
53574
CKBooksPublishing.com

To Hilary and Eric,
who have endured so many stories

"The fool doth think he is wise, but the wise man knows himself to be a fool."

~ *As You Like It*
William Shakespeare

CONTENTS

SAVING EUNICE

Eunice, the sylph-like girl in Wayne's aerobics class, reminded him of a graceful gazelle he'd seen on an African travel documentary. She always wore black—never fuchsia, lime, or tangerine shorts and halters like the other girls. Her lovely face had a dark quality, too, with deep brown eyes and a pale face framed by chocolate-brown hair.

Black made Eunice look older than her mid-twenties, in Wayne's opinion. At thirty-seven, he was at least a decade older than Eunice. Because she was so serious, Wayne suspected Eunice was the type who preferred older men. Based on her precisely-executed aerobic moves, he figured Eunice might be a stickler for organizing every minute aspect of her life, too. Just like him.

Someday Wayne intended to summon his courage and talk to Eunice like Steve did in aerobics class. Steve, a rock-solid specimen of bulging muscles, was the only one who could coax Eunice to laugh. "Our lady in black again today," he'd say, flashing that captivating smile punctuated with deep dimples. "Looking good, pretty girl Eunice."

"Oh. Thanks." She'd blush, raise her delicate eyebrows, and smile.

Wayne thought God must have created Eunice's voice for his angel chorus. It was soft like cotton and soothing like a warm bath towel. At night, he lay perfectly still on a narrow bed in the little trailer he called home. He'd crimp his eyes shut and pretend Eunice was saying loving words to him in her lush voice.

In aerobics class Wayne had figured out a way to study Eunice without her knowing. He positioned himself before a wall of mirrors, pulled a baseball cap brim low over his thick eyeglasses, and watched Eunice in a row behind him.

A couple of times Wayne had tried to follow Eunice home after aerobics class. She always parked her old, green Honda, with its dent in the right front fender, at the far end of the fitness club lot. So he parked his battered, gray Chevy the opposite direction. Even though his old car shone from Wayne's constant polishing, he figured Eunice was less apt to notice a gray car than she would have the red convertible he coveted.

Following Eunice had proven tricky. Left out of the parking lot. Right onto a frontage road. A sharp turn onto the highway. She drove fast and erratically, unlike her smooth and rhythmic aerobic moves. This aspect of Eunice signaled something promising to Wayne about her personality. Maybe she was more of an adventurous risk-taker than the introvert she seemed to be in aerobics class.

The first time Wayne followed Eunice, she'd escaped

on the highway. He had cursed the pickup truck that pulled between their cars and allowed her to vanish. The second time, he'd tailed her more closely, hiding behind oversized, dark glasses. Still, she'd managed to elude him.

Each time, Wayne had documented Eunice's route the same way he did his other daily details—with yellow Post-it notes. A series of Post-its, arranged exactly one-half inch apart, lined his Chevy dashboard.

Wayne had envisioned the perfect setting in which a woman who wore only black, and was well-organized, might reside. A sleek apartment. Skylights streaming sunshine. Contemporary furniture. Polished wood floors. He imagined Eunice placing her tennis shoes inside the front door on a mat purchased just for them. In her kitchen of stainless steel and black granite, she might select a china teacup from a symmetrical lineup. Or she might clip magazine couture ads with rail-thin women wearing black and maybe even use Post-it notes to organize them.

Wayne's own living quarters consisted of a single, long, narrow space. He had measured the square footage over and over so that his few furniture items sat equidistant from one another. He'd organized his kitchen cupboards as methodically as he did merchandise on the shelves at Curly's Convenience Store, where he worked weekends. Walls of his trailer were blanketed in yellow Post-its, transforming drab brown surfaces to a lemon hue. And though there was nothing valuable to steal, he had two padlocks on the trailer door.

One Friday night as Wayne lay in bed thinking about that day's aerobics class and Eunice, he had a potent fantasy. She was tiptoeing toward him past orderly stacks of cardboard boxes crammed into his small living quarters. Lights from his trailer park, shining through the window, provided a backdrop for her apparition. The whites of her eyes glistened above her flickering smile. Her cheeks were flushed as she crooked a finger to beckon him. "Hi, Wayne," she said with a trilling emphasis on the W.

Wayne shuddered with excitement and a new resolve. He had to succeed in his pursuit of Eunice. Monday, three days from now, was going to be the day he was victorious. He intended to run red lights and let the speedometer climb to eighty if that was what it would take to follow Eunice home and introduce himself.

By Saturday morning Wayne was giddy with anticipation about next Monday's plan. He put on his jeans and headed for Curly's Convenience Store. Wayne's only other income came from doing odd jobs at the fitness club, which gave him free aerobics classes as partial pay. But Wayne was so short of cash that he owned just two sets of clothes—his baggy exercise sweat suit worn with a leather belt and his work outfit of ragged jeans with his dad's holey T-shirt that said, "I'D RATHER BE FISHING."

Curly had reprimanded Wayne after his first few times at work. "No need to put them soup cans or razor blades in perfect lines on the shelf," Curly had said. "This job ain't like arranging pins in the bowling alley."

Still, Wayne had persisted in organizing cough drops, toothpaste, shaving cream, bottled drinks, and more in even and parallel rows.

So Curly had confronted Wayne again, "You're driving me nuts, boy, with everything having to be just so. But good help is hard to find. So if you wanta take your time and do it perfect, fine. But I'm only paying you for eight hours a day."

Some days Wayne worked twelve hours, not eight. Even as a young boy, he'd needed absolute order. After he'd spent several days arranging his stuffed animals in a perfect row, then counting them incessantly and refusing to stop, his mom consulted the doctor. Afterward, she'd said, "Wayne, some people are just different from normal ones. They have to do things over and over. You can't help being the way you are."

When Mom had taken off to escape Dad, Wayne lost the only person who made him feel it was okay to be so different.

By noon Saturday Wayne had finished stacking Milky Way and Snickers candy bars in their separate rows. He went to the store's makeshift, back-room lunch quarters—a card table set amidst piles of merchandise. Curly allowed each employee one free sandwich daily.

Munching on his ham and cheese, Wayne noticed a girly magazine someone had left open on the table. A female with lips that appeared smeared with Crisco stared back at Wayne and conjured a horrible adolescent memory.

One day he'd come across Dad's stacked magazines of nearly-naked girls in racy poses hidden in their garage. He was eyeing a voluptuous girl in a skimpy swimsuit when he'd heard, "Wayne, where are you?" Dad had come home from his car mechanics job early. Magazines had tumbled out of Wayne's hands and flown all over the oil-streaked garage floor.

Even now his heart still surged at the thought of Dad pummeling him with the thick belt Wayne wore nowadays to aerobics class.

When Wayne was in his twenties, Dad had died in an auto accident. That was the happiest day of Wayne's life. He had taken the small amount of money Dad left and bought himself a trailer. And when he moved there, Wayne had taken only three mementos of Dad—his belt, his magazines, and his T-shirt.

After his convenience store lunch, Wayne headed for the shelf of potato chips he needed to organize. That task always frustrated Wayne since the bags kept falling onto each other and looked messy. Then he heard a man up at the cashier counter say, "Hey, how's it going?"

Wayne knew that voice. It was Steve, flirting with Amy the cashier. Panicked that Steve might see him and maybe tell Eunice where he worked, Wayne fled to the back room. After delaying as long as possible, he returned. Steve had left.

Sidling up to Amy, Wayne said, "Do you know that guy who was just in here?"

Amy, who had tattoos wrist-to-neck, grinned and said, "Nope but he's one hot dude." She eyed Wayne's stringy hair and stout frame. "Make you jealous?"

On Monday afternoon, five minutes before aerobics class was to end, Wayne saw Eunice consult her black watch. She picked up her fitness ball and tiptoed to the sidelines. After stashing her equipment in the storage room, she took a black hooded jacket from a coat hook and headed out.

Wayne raised his hand, motioned to Mary the instructor, and contorted his face in fake pain while clutching his stomach. She returned a look of concern and flicked her fingers at him in dismissal. He left his fitness ball in place, grabbed his worn, wool jacket, dashed from the room, mounted the stairs two at a time, bolted through the lobby, and nearly fell as he stumbled over a child's discarded toy truck.

In the frigid late afternoon air outside, Wayne saw Eunice's black silhouette hurrying to her car. Though he always counted the usual seventy-some steps from the lobby to his car, today that wouldn't work as he slid across the icy pavement. He waited until Eunice exited the parking lot before accelerating and heading out. He stayed close behind her, counting on his dark glasses and baseball cap to camouflage his face.

As Eunice alternated between slamming on her brakes and accelerating without warning, Wayne resisted an urge to honk his horn to stop her. Driving so recklessly on ice might endanger her life.

After twenty minutes of following Eunice's zigzag route, Wayne was relieved when she turned onto a quiet street of modest bungalows. Trails of smoke curled out of their chimneys to form artistic patterns in the sky. Small squares of earth, once green with summer grass, lay like blocks of frosted ice in front of each small house. Naked branches of trees, raped of leaves by winter winds, formed an arch under which Eunice's Honda traveled. Finally, she slowed down and turned onto a driveway with narrow, twin, concrete ribbons, then disappeared into her attached garage.

Wayne inched his Chevy to the curb across the street. It was getting dark and he already felt chilled to the bone. He focused on Eunice's house until an interior light shone through lacy curtains at a front room window.

A couple of hours had passed by the time Wayne—his hands nearly frozen in his lap—awoke with a start from a nap. He blew on his fingers to revive them. Dark had painted the neighborhood with an inky brush. In Eunice's house, several lights were on. Huddled behind the steering wheel, Wayne realized that he hadn't formulated a plan beyond finding out where Eunice lived. He needed to think and was famished. Images of hamburgers danced across his mind. He started the car and headed back toward a street where he'd sighted a giant hamburger sign flashing on a tall pole.

At the restaurant he ordered a double burger with the works, French fries, and a chocolate shake. The restaurant, full of screaming kids chasing around, was the type of chaotic place that made Wayne nervous. He rushed to a back booth to escape them.

There he devoured the burger and slurped the shake. Last came the French fries, which he counted and arranged in parallel rows on paper napkins before dunking each one in ketchup.

Over and over Wayne had vowed to give up junk food. He'd gained twenty pounds from the convenience store's ice cream and candy bars. And he'd become addicted to peanut M&M's. Truthfully, he didn't mind being so heavy except when it came to Eunice. He knew she wouldn't want an overweight boyfriend.

In the restaurant's warmth, he began to think more clearly about how to introduce himself to Eunice. At her front door, he might say, "A delivery for Miss Eunice . . ." But he didn't know her last name. Maybe he could pound at the door, screaming about some neighborhood crisis and that Eunice must come with him.

Someone had left behind plastic silverware encased in a paper ring, which he removed and twirled on his pinky finger. Wayne imagined it transformed to a metal ring.

"Let the circle be unbroken," he sang, tapping the table with another finger as the paper spun. "Let the circle . . ."

"Man, look at that dude over there," a kid in the booth across from Wayne said to his companion. "Wacko." The boy flashed his middle finger as they got up and left.

Wayne examined the paper circle and creased a portion of it to create a smaller size to fit Eunice's finger. He extended it to his imaginary companion across the table.

"Eunice, I want you to, I mean, would you consider . . ." His heart swelled as the word "marry" dangled on the tip of his tongue.

Wayne's Chevy crept back onto Eunice's block and stopped at the exact spot where he'd parked before. Someday he intended to visit her in that red convertible or a sleek Porsche. By then he planned to live in a fancy apartment and have a sculpted body like Steve. In his car there would be a tiny box with an enormous silver bow on the leather car seat beside him.

He turned off the ignition and inhaled deeply. His lungs gagged at the intake of Arctic air. It made him think of his frosty bed in his trailer and slipping beneath sheets that felt like they'd been packed in snow. Sometimes he pretended that Eunice was in bed with him. He imagined her warmth, the curve of her bare shoulder, and the silk straps of her nightgown. Now, looking at her house, he began to throb at the thought of being with the real Eunice before the night was over.

Eunice's front porchlight flashed on. Then lights flickered in Wayne's rear view mirror. A car careened onto Eunice's driveway. The wheels must have hit a patch of ice because the car slid off the concrete ribbons onto frozen grass. The driver cut his lights. But no one exited the car.

Wayne envisioned the visitor as an elderly version of Eunice—her mother, who walked with a cane and needed extra time to leave a car, or a girlfriend, who was finishing a phone call before dashing to the house.

Finally, a tall, shadowy figure emerged from the car and wrestled with several shopping bags. One bag fell and slid toward the sidewalk. Wayne rolled down his window. As the figure raced for the errant bag, his body was camouflaged by a billowing trench coat. But when light from a street lamp washed over the man's face, Wayne saw the unmistakable square jaw and shock of black hair.

It was Steve.

As Steve reached the front porch, Eunice came out, opened her arms, and embraced him. He kissed the top of her head before they went inside.

Tears welled in Wayne's eyes. How could Eunice betray him with Steve? She seemed so shy that it had not occurred to Wayne she might have a boyfriend. Wayne decided he had to see inside Eunice's house to calculate his next move.

He slid on an ice patch and nearly fell on his way to her front windows. Standing on tiptoes, he was able to look inside through cutouts in the curtain fabric. Peering through the lacy holes reminded him of the first time he'd looked into a kaleidoscope at spaces interspersed with explosions of purple, black, and green. But he couldn't see the room clearly and circled the house in hopes of finding windows with better views.

Next door a dog barked ferociously. Wayne moved toward the back of Eunice's house, hoping to quiet the howling beast. A light flashed on in Eunice's back room. He crept toward its window, which had sheer curtains that made it easy to see two people—Eunice and Steve.

Eunice had put on a fuzzy, red robe that appeared to float around her. Steve had stripped to boxer shorts. Thick hair blanketed his bare chest below broad shoulders. They kissed and groped, bobbing up and down like apples in a Halloween water tub. Steve ran his hand over Eunice's hair, down her back, and inside her open robe. She stroked his cheek, then ducked to kiss his stomach.

Wayne gasped for air. He willed the two of them to stop. Eunice squealed behind the window glass as Steve laughed.

Wayne hunkered down against the house foundation and considered his options. Steve was so powerfully built and Eunice so dainty that he was afraid she might get hurt.

He got up again, balanced on tiptoes, and peeked in. Steve's hands were moving even more frantically over Eunice's body. She flung her head back and moaned as Steve slipped the robe off her shoulders.

"Stop it!" Wayne whispered as he gaped at Eunice's

beautiful naked body. But Steve was like a madman, squeezing and stroking and nipping at Eunice. As she struggled, Steve pushed her down onto the bed and fell on top of her.

"Stop it!" Wayne muttered again. His frosty breath lingered on the night air as the dog next door resumed barking.

He raced toward the back porch. Its glass storm door was unlocked. Sagging boards squeaked as he moved across the porch to jiggle the knob of a second door, which accessed the kitchen. Eunice had locked that one.

Wayne crossed his arms and heaved himself against the door. It failed to yield. He thought of Superman as he tried it a second time. His right shoulder missed its target and grazed the vertical glass panel beside the door. Glass splintered. Wayne felt a sharp stab in his upper arm. He couldn't see in the dark but sensed that blood was spurting like a geyser from his wound.

He suspected the door panel's smashed opening might be surrounded by jagged glass. Gingerly he inserted his arm through the opening to locate the interior door handle and unlock it. The gash in his arm throbbed.

Then Wayne thought of Eunice inside, and his pain lessened. She would bandage his cuts, coo over his bloody condition, and make that low guttural groan of desire he'd heard through the window. Once she saw that he had come to rescue her, Eunice would realize Wayne loved her more than Steve ever could.

Wayne twisted the knob and the kitchen door creaked open. He blinked in dense blackness, felt his way along a wall while counting the steps, and bumped into a stove. Blood was trickling down his arm. His legs threatened to buckle, and his heart pounded.

"Eunice, I'm coming," he whispered, making baby steps into dark nothingness.

A step sounded on the kitchen floor. Wayne froze. It creaked again.

Blood was traveling faster down his arm now. Sparklers, the Fourth of July kind, shimmered behind his eyelids. He inhaled deeply. The rasp of his breath sliced through the darkness.

"Eunice, I'm here to save you," he called.

The slam of something against his temple made Wayne careen sideways. A shrill scream sounded nearby.

"Eunice!" Wayne heard his voice rise from the floor and echo off the walls. "I'm coming."

A Christmas Dream

Lights flashed on the miniature Christmas tree pinned to the lapel of Hilda's drab work smock. Red. Green. Red. Green. Her lank, gray hair hung over a drugstore customer's package of chewing gum and a pregnancy test kit.

Hilda's muddy brown eyes studied the teenager's anxious face. "Happy holidays to you, missy. Didn't get yourself in the family way now, did you, honey?"

The girl, wearing a worn, tan sweatshirt embossed "Milburn High Cougars," had freckles and a turned-up nose. She shrugged and averted Hilda's gaze.

The heartbreak and angst lacing the teenager's face propelled Hilda back to her own school days as an outcast alone at a cafeteria table, chunky and orphaned, desperate for reassurance and affection.

"Well, try to have a merry Christmas anyway." Hilda patted the girl's hand.

Behind the teen fidgeting shoppers cleared their throats, glared at Hilda, and glanced at wrist watches.

One wrestled with a screaming baby. "Jingle Bells" wafted through the store to collide with Salvation Army chimes jangling near the front door.

Hilda spotted the tall man who'd recently caused her legs to quiver at first sight. His gentle expression, soft eyes, and friendly smile reminded her of a teacher she'd idolized in fifth grade. Her heart had swelled when that teacher complimented her, just as it had when the tall man studied her name tag and said, "Hilda, have a nice day."

Now, he placed toothpaste, breath mints, and a box of condoms on her counter and held out cash. "Hilda, I love your Christmas tree with those blinking lights."

"Love?" Her hand flew to the tree before realizing he would see her chewed fingernails, dotted with red flecks resembling chipped paint.

The customer behind him said, "Christ, I always get in the wrong line."

"Shouldn't say the name of our Lord that way." Hilda frowned at the guy.

"I wouldn't hafta if you'd do your job fast instead of moving like a snail."

"It's my fault," the tall man said. "At Christmastime people should be kind."

Hilda canvassed his left hand for a wedding ring but found none. The image of a girlfriend, blond and curvy, flashed through her mind.

The tall man twirled car keys. "Hilda, get all those Christmas presents wrapped."

Hilda broke into a joyful smile and hummed a line from "God Rest Ye Merry Gentlemen," certain this divine man would love the Christmas gift she planned to bestow on him.

Three days before Christmas, Ruby, Hilda's Maine Coon cat, sneaked out of the bed they shared and hid. When Hilda found her inside a cupboard, Ruby refused to eat. Hilda cradled the bulky, limp cat and offered a spoon of cat food. "Mama can't go to work unless you eat something, sweetie."

A groan slipped from Ruby's mouth.

"Babykins, I can't leave you here all alone." She picked up Ruby, carried her to the bathroom, and wrapped her in a terry towel. "You're going to have to be so quiet, Ruby. No one must know you are at work. Especially Tory, my boss."

By the time Hilda had fiddled with the cat, she was late leaving. There was no time for applying makeup or styling her hair.

Beads of perspiration dotted Hilda's upper lip as she hurried into the drugstore and raced, with Ruby in a large paper shopping bag, to counter one. Tory Adams, the new manager, had turned on "Frosty the Snowman" at a volume that made Hilda's head pound.

She tucked the shopping bag beneath her counter and pushed her knees against it, hoping Ruby would be comforted by the scent of Hilda nearby. Hilda offered frantic prayers to the speckled ceiling: "Please let Ruby be quiet. And keep Tory away from us." She and the know-it-all manager had already clashed when Hilda's cash register came up short one recent evening.

Every customer that day seemed grumpy or agitated. A scruffy teenage boy bristled when Hilda asked if he was old enough to buy cigarettes. His age made her think of the pregnant teen, and she hoped that the baby's father was not a questionable type, like this one.

A frazzled mother, with a toddler whose nose stream-ed snot, broke five candy canes as she slammed them down in frustration.

"Meow. Meow." From the depths of her paper bag, Ruby called to Hilda.

"Mommy, want a cat for Christmas." The toddler imi-tated a meow sound.

"Stop making that noise, Andrew. I've told you twenty times that Mommy is allergic to cats." She sneezed. "Any-way, they're sneaky. Dogs are better."

Ruby called out again as if to protest the insult.

Hilda amplified her words, hoping to drown the ris-ing tide of Ruby's displeasure. "You're wrong about cats, ma'am."

By afternoon Hilda's back ached, and her knees felt numb from pressing against Ruby's bag. During a lull in the stream of shoppers, she'd slipped cat treats below the counter. Ruby had rewarded her with a contented sigh. Hilda worried the poor thing might suffocate down in that bag all tangled in her towel.

The tall man's deep voice reverberated nearby in a lineup of customers. He'd be gazing at Hilda in moments, and the prospect made her long to dive beneath the counter. She knew her face probably looked scary with no makeup, and she cringed at the thought of him seeing her this way.

After the man's last visit, Hilda decided to name him David. The only David she'd known was a neighborhood boy, who was kind and didn't notice her shabby clothes.

Suddenly, David stood before her. "Hilda, where's your lighted Christmas tree pin?"

"Oh, I forgot. I promise to wear it tomorrow." She yearned to tell him Ruby might be sick and she didn't know what to do, that Tory could come flying over any minute and maybe even fire her. She imagined relaxing with David near a lavishly decorated Christmas tree, confiding her woes, and resting her head in his lap as he stroked her hair.

"It's Christmas Eve day after tomorrow, Hilda," David said. "Maybe I'll see you then."

At closing time Hilda was locking her cash register when Tory charged up. "Stop at my office on your way out." He disappeared as if an apparition.

Hilda figured someone complained she was too slow or reported Ruby's whines. "I cannot tolerate this," she could hear him say. She pictured herself on a sidewalk bench, snow falling on her shoulders, destitute and scared on Christmas Eve.

As she lifted Ruby's bag and tried to act nonchalant like it contained Yule gifts, Hilda scanned the store for a place to hide the cat. A plaintive meow rose from the bag.

"Shh." Hilda darted past a customer studying rows of deodorant.

The woman twisted around. "You got a cat in that bag?"

"Merry Christmas." Hilda raced away. Her eyes swept the aisles. The bag would never fit behind tidy rows of hair spray, sleep aids, or cotton balls. It had to be away from the pharmacy section. Otherwise, someone might hear Ruby as they waited for antidotes to lower blood pressure or decongestants to ease breathing.

Down aisle seven she spotted mounds of bagged garden soil. Hiding Ruby behind them would be perfect. Who would consider planting tulips when snow was on the ground? Hilda raced down aisle seven, put down her bag, wrestled with the five-pound sacks, created an opening, and slid in her bag. "I'll be back soon, love," Hilda whispered.

Tory's office reminded Hilda of her dismal life. No windows. A battered desk shoved against a wall with peach paint flakes on the floor. One dilapidated swivel chair at an odd angle to the desk. Cardboard boxes piled in a corner. Dim lights over it all.

"Hill-duh." Tory pronounced her name as if speaking to a senile person.

Though his work badge said "Mr. Adams," Hilda never knew what to call him since he was young enough to be her son. She thought he fit the definition of a twerp. "Yes?" Her eyes strayed to the ceiling, then down to his soiled tennis shoes.

"Hill-duh, I don't know what's goin' on, but you have been actin' pretty weird."

"Weird?"

"Yeah. Ya know, like you're on drugs or somethin'. Talkin' so loud I could hear ya across the store. Lookin' around all the time like the cops are after ya."

Hilda squared her shoulders. "Young man, I've never taken drugs in my life."

"Cool it. Just kiddin'." He scratched his oily hair, producing flakes of dandruff. "Ya gotta act more normal. Like Mary Sue on counter two. Customers want somebody who's not weird."

"Stop using that word."

"Okay. Strange. A person who's not strange." Tory yawned. "Got my message? I'm about to lock up so get your stuff pronto."

Hilda detoured down aisle seven, pulled out Ruby's bag, and stifled a shriek.

Ruby was gone.

That evening the sky looked ominous as Hilda, agonizing about how to rescue Ruby, trudged up three flights to her efficiency apartment and plopped onto her lumpy sofa. Still wearing her galoshes and holey scarf, she came up with an idea. The former store manager, who liked Hilda, had given her a key and the security alarm code. She got up, grabbed a flashlight and the key, and left.

In the shadowy alley, Hilda unlocked the store's door and entered a code on an illuminated security panel. Immediately a screeching siren blasted inside the store. Hilda froze in terror. Tory must have changed the code.

Hilda knew she should flee before the police or Tory showed up, but her feet, as if set in cement, refused to move. She struggled to catch her breath and entertained visions of her mug shot on the newspaper's front page.

Before long a burly cop raced toward Hilda. Behind him came Tory.

"Hill-duh, I should fire you." Tory glared. "I told ya to stop doin' weird stuff."

"She works here?" The cop eyed Hilda's coat with safety pins replacing buttons.

"I can explain." Hilda trembled. "I left my purse in the store and needed it."

"Go get it. Fast," Tory said. "Officer, sorry to bother you. She's just weird."

In the store Hilda raced up and down aisles whispering, "Scooby Ruby, come to Mama. Where are you, baby girl?" Ruby remained sequestered somewhere in the store.

All night Hilda was awake picturing Ruby injured after a display of glass perfume bottles collapsed on top of her or a pyramid of Coke cans buried her.

Near dawn she decided to try and make a better impression on Tory so as not to get fired. She applied all the makeup she had splurged on recently to make herself look pretty for David. At her bathroom mirror, milky face foundation spread across her face like soft butter on grainy toast. Dark brown eyebrow pencil made her straggly brows resemble melted chocolate. Inky mascara turned her eyelashes into thick clumps. She fixed her hair in a bun and attached a plaid bow, then doused herself with cologne from an atomizer swiped from the drugstore.

As Hilda entered the store, "Joy to the World" blared and accompanied her as she traversed the aisles calling "Scooby Ruby?"

"Hill-duh!" Tory came around a corner. He looked at Hilda's garish face, raised his eyebrows, and shook his head. "Better shape up today or else."

Right after lunch, which Hilda had spent searching for Ruby, a woman with bright red hair ran toward counter one yelling, "I thought this store had a no-pets policy! There's a huge cat in the candy aisle."

As Hilda headed toward the boxed chocolates and mints section, she collided with Tory, who was carrying Ruby in a stranglehold.

"Damn cat, Humane Society here you come!" Tory bellowed.

A woman in the small group gathered near Tory said, "That's hardly the Christmas spirit, cursing an innocent cat."

"I adore cats." Hilda held out her arms. "I'll take her."

"Is anybody working here?" a disgruntled customer called from up front.

"Hill-duh, didn't I warn—" As Tory pointed a finger at Hilda, Ruby broke loose. She fell to the floor and hurried to rub her body against Hilda's leg.

"Go ahead and take the stupid cat, Hill-duh. Just get it out of sight right now."

Hilda rushed to her counter and put Ruby in the shopping bag.

That night, jubilant about Ruby's return, Hilda sat with the cat and planned David's gift presentation tomorrow on Christmas Eve. She could say, "David, I realize we don't know each other very well, but Ruby and I would like to invite you—" No, that wouldn't do. He had no idea who Ruby was. "Are you going to be alone for Christmas? Please join us for dinner. I hope you like ham." That'd be better.

Ruby, who'd been shadowing Hilda as if she might vanish, stretched a thick paw across her owner's thigh. Hilda stroked the cat's dense fur and imagined her own fingers exploring David's handsome face. "Ruby, darling, you'll have to behave yourself when David comes. He will love you, I know."

On Christmas Eve, Santa stood at Hilda's counter with a bottle of mouthwash chortling, "Ho, ho, ho!"

"Daddy. Santa!" A little girl in a ballerina skirt jumped up and down.

"Merre-eee Chrisss-muss." Santa whipped a piece of candy shaped like a reindeer from his pocket and handed it to the child.

Santa leaned close to Hilda. "Gotta keep my breath fresh for the young tots." The scent of whiskey streaming from his mouth made her tip backward.

"Why, if it isn't Santa Claus!" David stepped up and shook his hand. "You must be on your way to the North Pole."

Hilda trembled at the sight of David and touched one of her scarlet cheeks.

David retreated after a whiff of Santa's breath. "Been to a party?"

Hilda spotted Tory watching her long line of customers. "Santa, time to leave and get presents ready to deliver." She stammered, "David, I—"

A customer behind David stepped in front of him. "I'm in a big hurry."

"Go ahead of me." David clutched a stack of decorated Christmas cookie tins.

"Thank you, David," Hilda said.

He flashed a crooked grin. "David? That's not my name."

As the man she'd dubbed David waited, Hilda rehearsed her invitation. She would have to deliver it fast.

Just before Hilda finished with the customer in a hurry, Mary Sue opened counter two. "Next in line, right here," she pronounced as if a carnival barker.

As David switched to Mary Sue's queue, Tory rushed up. His wild eyes darted between Hilda and Mary Sue. "Speed it up, girls! Folks got lots of Christmas junk to do besides standing around waiting on you slowpokes."

"David?" Hilda cursed the quake in her voice as she pleaded for his attention.

Hilda's customer swiveled toward David at Mary Sue's counter. "Hey, you with the cookie deals, the dame here wants to talk to you."

David turned around and lost control of his tins, which rolled across the floor.

"Me?" He looked toward Hilda.

A thick clot rose in Hilda's throat, threatening to silence her. "I, uh, could you please stop over here before you leave?"

"I'm already late."

"It's Christmas Eve."

"Okay, Hilda. Just for a minute, after I pick up my tins."

"Hill-duh!" Tory had reappeared. "Remember our conversation about actin' weird, I mean, strange? Now, you're bein' strange in a different way. Chill out. Got it?"

She nodded dully as the tall man approached to ask, "Hilda, what did you want?"

His mint-drenched breath floated into her nostrils as she said, "David, I mean—"

"My name is Lyle, not David." He looked puzzled. "Friends call me Lie." He winked and grinned.

"Oh no, Lie doesn't suit you." She attempted the invitation again. "I was wondering, you see, I mean, would you, what are you doing . . . ?" She exhaled and felt her ribs contract. "What are you doing for Christmas?"

"Tomorrow?" His voice resembled a modulated melody. It was that tone Hilda's doctor used with her. "Christmas Day?"

Hilda smiled and envisioned her red paper tablecloth, a pair of green candles from the bargain shelf on aisle three, and Ruby wearing her "I'm A Christmas Angel" halo.

"Tomorrow? Why, Hilda, I'm not sure."

Hilda's heart did pirouettes. She saw him at her festive table lifting a glass of cranberry juice to toast Christmas, her, and Ruby. "Then you can—"

"I have business matters that will take me out of the city tomorrow."

"Business? On Christmas Day?" She heard her voice rise, tremble on the edge of a steep cliff, and fall like a meteor. "But Ruby and I—"

"Hill-duh!" Tory's voice rose and enveloped her.

Lyle looked toward Tory. "Have a wonderful Christmas, Hilda."

"Or maybe you could come the day after," Hilda whispered as she watched the tall man, balancing cookie tins in his arms, walk with measured steps out the front door.

It was nearly lunch time, and Hilda was wiping away tears with a Kleenex when she heard the girl's wavering voice.

"If you were pregnant and all alone, you'd really have something to cry about."

Hilda looked into the freckled face of the girl who'd bought a pregnancy kit.

"My foster mom kicked me out today cuz of the

baby." The girl's hand shook as she held out a dollar and a candy bar.

Hilda said, "Honey, a growing baby needs more than candy for lunch" as she thought, *Oh no, not foster care!* She lowered her voice, eyeing Tory across the room. "Meet me by the aspirin section in five minutes."

While waiting on a well-dressed man buying tree ornaments, Hilda thought about the coincidence of this pregnant girl ending up in foster care just as she had years before.

In third grade Hilda had been called out of class to hear that her mother, a single nurse who doted on her only child, died in a car crash. Hilda had never known a father, her mother having dismissed his existence with vague references to his mysterious death.

After enduring several foster care placements, Hilda was all too familiar with the downgrading and uncertainty of her altered life. She'd gone from new clothes to hand-me-downs, and praise to neglect.

By high school she'd lost interest in studies and dropped out. Ever since, Hilda had supported herself with dead-end jobs and tried online dating services to meet someone. A couple of men had agreed to have coffee. Afterward, Hilda never heard from them. She knew her cats—Ruby and others before her—were hardly substitutes for romance. But at least most cats didn't reject you like the man she'd named David had.

At the aspirin display, Hilda said to the girl, "I don't know your name."

"Angie."

"There's a coffee shop next door, Angie. Let me grab my coat and we'll go."

"I have to go to my after-school job."

"Angie, do you like ham? And cats?"

"Ham, so-so. I love cats though."

"Somehow I just knew you would, my dear. Ruby and I would be so happy if you joined us for Christmas dinner."

"Who's Ruby?"

"My wonderful cat. When I found Ruby on a sidewalk, she was all alone and frightened with no one to turn to, sort of like you and me."

The girl broke into a tentative smile, transforming her face from sullen to sweet.

Hilda smiled back at her. "But now you have us. Ruby and me."

The Collector

Mitzi clipped the newspaper coupon as carefully as if it were a priceless photo. Ten dollars off a fifty-dollar purchase at Miller's Department Store. She ran an arthritic finger over another ad offering 30 percent savings on winter items at Wilke's Wearables. She cut it out next, envisioning Agnes in a green, fur-trimmed parka. Her sister's birthday was next week, and a jacket to match Agnes's green eyes would be a wonderful surprise. Mitzi planned to stage an extravagant party for Agnes to lure her for a long overdue visit.

The kitchen clock read six-thirty a.m. That left two hours to search for more coupons and then dress up for her daily shopping excursion. Mitzi took a sip of instant coffee and glanced at the kitchen counters. Velvet pouches of costume jewelry and small cardboard boxes holding watches, necklaces, and bracelets covered the Formica surfaces. In precarious piles on the floor were large boxes containing Kentucky-Derby-caliber hats trimmed with feathers, lace, and fake flowers.

It was miraculous that the waist-high stacks of boxes, which zigzagged through the house, did not tumble. Mitzi's Milwaukee bungalow had begun to grumble about all this excess. Not that the old house could talk, of course. But yesterday the door of her jammed coat closet had refused to shut. None of the other closet doors would close either.

Mitzi poked a ragged fingernail into her fire-engine-red hair. Clairol dye, purchased with a coupon, had promised a soft hue to cover her thin, gray hair. She'd hoped red tresses would make her resemble Agnes. Mommy had always said that Agnes's glorious hair made her the most beautiful of her two daughters.

"Miller's and Wilke's, here I come," Mitzi hummed. She put the coupons in a tidy stack before heading to her bedroom down a narrow hall lined with piles of merchandise.

While dressing each morning, Mitzi imagined she was about to audition for a movie role. She picked eye-catching colors, slathered on heavy makeup, and donned one of her wigs. Today she decided to copy her idol, the late screen star Elizabeth Taylor. She put on a padded bra to make herself look busty. From a drawer packed with gaudy jewelry, she chose a ring and necklace with big fake diamonds. She outlined her eyes with ebony pencil and put on a black wig. Should anyone ask Mitzi her name, she'd say Liz.

At Miller's, Mitzi wheeled her small suitcase of

coupons into the coat department. It was a nuisance to haul luggage as if she were about to move. But who knew when one of her hundreds of coupons might be needed? She stopped at a rack of sale parkas. Agnes had always loved bright colors like the scarlet hue of one hanging there. Mitzi hailed a salesclerk, waved her coupon, and asked, "Thirty percent off these coats, right?"

The skinny man scanned Mitzi's garish face, rotund frame, and plastic galoshes before saying icily, "These parkas are already reduced. The coupon is for regular prices."

"What! Downright false advertising," Mitzi blurted. "You just lost a very good customer."

Muttering, she headed out of Miller's to visit Wilke's at the other end of the mall.

At Wilke's, Mitzi had to haul her suitcase up steps to the second floor. A security guard blocked her path at the top. He eyed the suitcase. "What's in there?"

"A dead body." Mitzi tried to move around him.

"Don't get smart with me, lady." He pointed. "Open it."

As Mitzi flung open the top, coupons swirled out like snowflakes. "Now, look what you've done. I'll have to organize these by category all over again," she said.

That evening as Mitzi unpacked the parka she'd bought her sister at Wilke's, images of a six-year-old Agnes paraded by. Agnes giggling in a swimsuit. Blowing bubbles with her gum. Hugging her baby doll.

As kids the sisters had played dress-up in the attic with Mommy's old clothes. Mitzi had a crystalline memory of the day she and Agnes mapped out their adult futures as raindrops pelted the windows. Mitzi was wearing Mommy's burgundy wool blazer with a straw hat. Agnes had put on their mother's white ruffled blouse and a bright pink sweater with jeweled buttons. She'd flung a fluffy scarf about her shoulders to top it off.

"I'm going to be a princess when I grow up," Agnes had declared. A smile had spread across her heart-shaped face.

"You're already one," said Mitzi, studying her sister's translucent skin, which accentuated her beauty. "I'm going to be like Mommy and shop all the time."

Agnes had directed her dreamy expression to the rain outside. "Or maybe I'll be an angel. Then I can live in Heaven."

"You have to die to go up there," said Mitzi, who was seven. "You're only six."

"Will you come visit me if I die?" Agnes had asked in her sweet voice.

As Mitzi recollected that day, images of Agnes became wavy and gossamer-like. Agnes's eyes seemed to float away from her face as she disappeared into smoke. It made Mitzi feel hollow and scared.

"I can't wait to see you for your birthday, Agnes," she said.

The next morning as Mitzi clipped coupons, someone pounded on the front door. Then the doorbell chimed. But piles of boxes blocked the door. Best to ignore whoever it was, she decided. When knocking commenced at the kitchen door, a voice shouted, "You better let me in. It's your landlord!"

Mitzi visualized Lenny, the greasy-haired slob who rented her the bungalow several years ago. She hated the way his dark eyes darted furtively, like a rat. His breath was foul from cigarettes. But the place was cheap. And until now, he'd left her alone. "Coming," she yelled before maneuvering the path to the door between piles.

"Time to check up on you," Lenny said as Mitzi opened the door. "Came to see what kinda care you're taking of my joint."

"It's not a joint. And I'm taking perfect care of it," Mitzi said.

As he entered, Lenny's shoe struck a pyramid of boxes. They flew all directions and he yelled, "What the hell is all this stuff?"

"I do not allow swearing in my house, young man," Mitzi said. "Stop right now."

Lenny's eyes swept the mountains of merchandise. "Are you a nut case? Do you think I want my place to be a junk dump?"

"It is not junk." Mitzi opened a nearby closet and thrust a red dress with a rhinestone collar toward Lenny. "See? I buy only high quality."

"Kinda fancy duds for your type, ain't it?" He fingered the fabric. "Looks more like something my girlfriend would go for. Got more stuff like this?"

"My wardrobe is none of your business," Mitzi said. "Now, please leave."

"Just so ya know, I'll be back. So clean the place up." Lenny charged out.

Mitzi trembled with indignation. The nerve of him, barging in like a policeman bent on arresting a murderer. She would get even. And she was not about to move. She'd consult Agnes about it during their birthday gala. Somehow she had to keep Lenny out.

The daily bus that ferried Mitzi to her stores didn't go as far as Home Depot or Lowe's. So she headed to Walgreens, hoping their home supplies department might have what she needed—chains to stretch across the kitchen door as a barricade.

"Welcome to Walgreens, corner of healthy and happy, or however that goes," said a skinny boy with a nose ring.

"Young man, I'll be happy if you carry some thick, metal chain."

"Whoa, lady, you up to some mischief?" His grin revealed broken teeth. "You need Homer Depot." He snickered at his attempted joke.

Out on the street corner, Mitzi debated. She hated to use part of that week's grocery money for a cab. But Lenny was apt to reappear soon. She hailed a taxi.

The interior of Home Depot felt to Mitzi like a warehouse full of people on steroids. Giant machines beeped and moved huge cartons. An intercom blared messages. Customers scurried around to buy paint, nails, saws, and ladders. She spotted a stocky man in an orange Home Depot apron and raced toward him.

"I'm Al." He stroked a thick, white beard. "Follow me. Chains in aisle ten."

"Al, has anyone said you look like Santa Claus?" Mitzi asked as they walked.

"Sure 'nuf. Play him every year for the kiddos," he said. "If you don't mind my asking, what are you going to do with chains? Trying to keep out burglars?"

"Sort of," said Mitzi.

Back home Mitzi struggled to install her chains across the kitchen door. Such barricades made her think of Mommy, who'd kept a padlocked storeroom in their basement. The few times little Mitzi had gotten to peek in, that room seemed spooky with countless boxes piled floor-to-ceiling. Portable clothing racks held rows of dresses with paper price tags dangling in the air. She'd wondered whether Mommy was running a secret clothing store.

Most weekdays Mommy had left young Mitzi and Agnes with a babysitter. Before dinner she'd returned with armloads of packages and ordered the girls to wait while she hid the purchases in the storeroom so Daddy wouldn't know of her frivolous expenditures.

The source of Mommy's plentiful money had been a mystery, too. When she died, Mommy had left her assets to Mitzi, not Agnes. So Mitzi had begun buying her sister things like the fur-trimmed parka.

A couple of days after her chain installation, Mitzi approached home carrying numerous shopping bags. A red Corvette was parked at her curb. Leaning against the passenger door was Lenny. Cigarette smoke swirled about his curly hair. He yelled, "I lost my key and you need to let me in."

As Mitzi puzzled over why Lenny was suddenly showing up so often, she plotted how to flee. He made her feel panicky. Her kitchen chains worked only when she was indoors to attach them. If he saw the chains, he'd know she was thwarting him. If she told him to come back later, he'd refuse.

Then she remembered a movie where a criminal had evaded prison by staging an accident. Mitzi started to run fast, tripped, and pitched sideways on the grass. Shopping bags flew all over. "Ouch," she screamed in fake pain.

Lenny, cigarette dangling from his mouth, raced to Mitzi. "Are you okay?" He stared at her aghast. Her brown wig lay like a piece of raccoon fur on the grass. Her skirt was askew, revealing thick, pale thighs. Clothes and shoes spilled out of shopping bags as though a whirlwind had swept by.

"My ankle," moaned Mitzi. "I think it's broken."

Lenny whipped out his cell phone. "I'll call an ambulance."

"No, call my sister, Agnes." Mitzi gave him a number.

Lenny dialed, then frowned. "No such phone number."

A man walking his Irish setter came up and said, "Need some help?"

"If you can get me home, I'll have Agnes drive me to the doctor," Mitzi said.

The dog yipped as the men struggled to support Mitzi. Slowly they inched her down the sidewalk. At her front door, Mitzi said, "Lenny, I'm in too much pain for you to come in now." She hobbled inside and slammed the door.

After unpacking that day's bags of presents for Agnes, Mitzi's thoughts turned to details of the birthday party, which was tomorrow night. She set the table for two with turquoise Fiestaware plates, cut-glass goblets, braided napkin rings, and party hats to wear during their hot fudge sundae dessert. She planned to serve Agnes's favorite dishes—fried Spam, creamy mashed potatoes, and lime Jell-O salad.

What should she wear? After rejecting a purple suit and a brown shift as options, Mitzi thought of the red dress Lenny had admired. That would be quite festive. In the closet she searched hanger after hanger but the dress was not there. Maybe she'd transferred it elsewhere. A frantic search of other closets yielded no red dress. In the process, Mitzi noticed the purple suit was missing, too.

Not a soul ever entered Mitzi's house. And she didn't believe in ghosts. But then she thought of Lenny. Weird and unlikable, yes. But a thief? She'd lay a trap to find out.

Before setting off on her shopping excursion the next day, Mitzi draped two of Agnes's birthday gifts across dining room chairs—a white blouse with a ruffled collar and a bright pink sweater with big, glittering, jeweled buttons. She'd searched all over town to find the items that replicated Agnes's attic outfit. Now, they'd serve as a lure for Lenny or whoever else was entering her house.

Mitzi toyed with the idea of trying to spy from somewhere outdoors in the neighborhood to see the intruder. But her street was devoid of hiding places. So she planned to depart for shopping at her usual time, then return much earlier than was her routine to catch the thief off-guard.

Mid-afternoon Mitzi returned home with groceries for the night's big dinner. No sign of a red Corvette, and Agnes's blouse and sweater were still in the dining room. Apparently the thief had taken a day off. Mitzi decided to shower and then cook in her brand-new Ralph Lauren bathrobe before changing to a dress. In her guest room, she opened the bathrobe box. It was empty.

Myriad fears began to stalk Mitzi. Since Lenny hadn't taken the clothes from the dining room, maybe someone else had a key to her house. Perhaps he was even hiding there right now. Warily she tiptoed room to room. She peeked in closets, beneath beds, and behind the shower curtain. Nothing in the house appeared to be out of place. Finally, convinced that no one was there, Mitzi began cooking for Agnes's party.

By five-thirty the Spam had been fried and the potatoes whipped. Mitzi rushed to get dressed and be ready by six o'clock. She was sure Agnes would arrive then because Mommy had always insisted six was the mandatory dining hour.

But as the minutes ticked past—twenty, thirty, then a full hour—Mitzi felt an unwelcome memory surfacing. Over the years, she'd perfected the art of blotting it out and substituting her own version of events. This time, the memory refused to be banished.

Mitzi had been eight at the time. Mommy was sobbing so loudly that the minister had to raise his voice to be heard. "God took this precious child to be with him in Heaven," he was saying. Daddy, tears cascading down his cheeks, had gripped Mitzi's hand. Only later would he explain, "Mitzi, our darling Agnes won't be coming home from the hospital. She . . ." He had choked trying to say the rest.

After that Mitzi's parents had never mentioned Agnes again. Overnight her toys and clothes had disappeared. Her locked bedroom had only been opened when Mommy stockpiled more stuff she spent all day buying.

In her dining room, Mitzi paced round and round the party table. She felt dizzy, not from the circles but from her jumbled thoughts. Memory was tangled with reality, past with present.

She wondered, *How could I have imagined my sister alive all these years as though Agnes might walk through the door at any moment? How could I have built my life and hopes around a sister who doesn't even exist?*

On a shelf behind kitchen pans, Mitzi kept a bottle of whiskey. Rarely did she even think of it let alone drink some. Now, she headed for the cupboard, hoping alcohol would slow her ricocheting thoughts. After pouring a generous glass, she moved past the dining room table, set for a party that would never happen, into the living room. Since its one chair and couch were piled with possessions, Mitzi plopped on the floor with her drink.

As she sipped, her mind began performing tricks again. She was playing hide-and-seek with Agnes, who appeared giggling one minute but vanished the next. Then Agnes's sweet childish face paraded by but it was attached to an adult body. Mitzi reached out to touch her sister. But her fingers felt only air.

At six the next morning, Mitzi sat up with a start. She was still on the living room floor, having slept there in her party clothes. Dark stains of spilled whiskey trailed down the front of her dress, and her stomach grumbled from no dinner the night before. She staggered to her feet and headed for the kitchen to fix instant coffee. One look at Spam left in the frying pan—now the texture of leather— reminded her of the aborted party. She had to escape the house and agonizing thoughts of Agnes. Too distracted to clip coupons from the morning paper, Mitzi rushed to change into shopping clothes.

By noon Mitzi had wandered through a dozen clothing stores without examining a single item. Exhaustion overwhelmed her. She longed to lie down, close her eyes, and make everything painful—past and present—disappear.

Near home Mitzi noticed a Corvette like Lenny's parked a few houses away from hers. She decided the time had come to tell him that these surprise visits had to end.

From the front hall, Mitzi heard a woman laughing. Mitzi removed her shoes in order to tiptoe quietly to the dining room, where the woman seemed to be.

"Baby, you're lookin' real good," she heard Lenny say.

"Like my fancy new frock?" a woman's voice asked.

As Mitzi rounded a corner into the dining room, a swirl of pink flashed by. A buxom brunette, dressed in Agnes's pink sweater and only underwear below it, was prancing about the dining room as though it were a burlesque stage.

Lenny was her audience, cheering her on with, "Hit it, baby girl!"

"Take off my sister's sweater right now," shouted Mitzi at the startled woman.

Lenny, for a change, was speechless. Finally, he said, "I was just showing Brenda some of your pricey clothes."

"I suppose you borrowed my new bathrobe, the red dress, and my purple suit to show Brenda, too," Mitzi said. "Now, get out of here, both of you, before I call the police."

Lenny sneered. "Why, I thought you'd call that sister of yours. Agnes. The one with a fake phone number. The one with all those unopened cards on your party table. The one whose sweater—"

"Shut up!" screamed Mitzi, covering her ears. "You don't know what it's like to have a wonderful sister who means the world to you. My sister, Agnes, lives very far away and has a good reason for never visiting me."

Mitzi lowered her voice. "I plan to go visit Agnes in that faraway place very soon, maybe later today."

THE MAMA MARY RAPIDS

"I hate marshmallows, Daddy." Artie eyed someone nearby toasting them over a campfire, then licked a thick finger smudged with chocolate. The teenager stared at his towering, lean father, Jim.

"Artie, how many times have I asked you to stop complaining and to call me Dad? Not Daddy." Jim ran a finger through thin, sandy hair.

Donny, Artie's sour-faced teenage brother, said, "Mommy, we want Twinkies, not marshmallows." Donny, wearing a T-shirt embossed with "WHATEVER," slouched in a canvas chair.

"Okay, boys." Their mother Rita, a bulky woman with a dark braid snaking down her back, struggled out of her chair. "I'll be right back with your Twinkies." She wore camouflage clothing and a sun protection hat that had a flap covering the back of her neck. She might have been setting off on a safari. She swatted a mosquito. "This part of camping sucks."

"Rita, no Twinkies for Artie and Donny." Jim pivoted toward his wife and scowled. "They don't need any more junk food."

"Since when have you been so interested in what our sons eat?" Rita spun around and headed off to their tent.

Watching his wife depart, Jim recalled the svelte and sweet-tempered Rita of their courtship days, who had now become pudgy and confrontational. He wondered why he agreed to come along on this rafting trip Rita had proposed. "For some family bonding," as she'd put it.

Four other campers, sitting by the fire in an opening surrounded by tents, had been listening to the squabbling Parsons family while basking in a late afternoon sun. This idyllic spot, a short walk from the picturesque river, was tucked into the woods. Inky dark evergreens interspersed with elegant white birch trees created a two-tone artistic backdrop behind the tents.

The campers had come to this pristine setting for the adventure of rafting its rapids, including a challenging one called Mama Mary. Legend was that its cascading waters were named for a high-spirited American Indian who had lived near the river.

One of the rafters, a platinum-haired woman named Lila, who wore orange shorts and a tight T-shirt, got up and fluffed her long curls with manicured red nails. The cloying gardenia scent of her perfume floated across the air as she winked at Jim. She motioned him to follow her behind a row of dense, tall bushes.

In the secluded area, Lila's soulful brown eyes swept Jim's face as her fingers brushed his chest. "My sweet Jimmy having more trouble in marital paradise with his Rita?"

Lila was short and stood on tiptoes to tickle Jim's neck. "I know how to make it better."

Jim kissed her cheek before pushing her fingers away. "I may not love my wife anymore but I'm not about to reveal our affair in front of her and my sons. You agreed to be discreet, remember? Don't let me down, baby."

Later, after dinner, newlywed Ryan Carson knelt inside his tent and eyed his red-headed bride Shelly. "Interesting group of rafters we have for tomorrow. How did that Jim end up with a fatso wife and two chubby, whining kids?"

"I heard Jim say he's a shrink." Shelly, who had light brown freckles scattered about her fair face, began to unbutton her blouse. "He seems kinda hip for an older guy. And how about Lila, that blond babe? She's smoking hot. She reminds me of a stalking panther when she walks. Something, body language maybe, tells me she and Jim knew each other before coming here. That kid of hers, Tony, is another spoiled brat."

"I can't see those sissy boys Donny and Artie riding river rapids." Ryan rolled his eyes. "Maybe their dad needs to do psychiatric work on his own family."

After a hearty breakfast of waffles and eggs the next morning, the rafters met with their leaders, Greg and Karen, for instruction about whitewater rafting. Greg, a muscular college student with an infectious smile, assigned Jim's family and the newlyweds to his raft. Karen, who sported pigtails and a lithe build, would steer the other passengers—Lila, her son Tony, and middle-aged sisters named Isabel and Helen.

At the rushing river the sparkling June sun reflected off the water, making it glitter in places like diamonds. Frothy waves, resembling swirls of whipped cream, crested over the rocks. It might have been a movie setting minus the actors.

Greg offered final instructions. "Please listen up, everyone." He repeated his list of rafting tips, waving tanned hands through the crisp air. When he finished, Greg turned toward Karen's raft where Lila's fifteen-year-old was hanging backward off its side. Greg pointed to him. "Tony, please don't do that."

"Throw out that bubble gum and sit up straight, Tony." Lila glared at her son.

"Cool it, Mom." Tony, whose broad shoulders and sculpted torso suggested an age beyond fifteen, spit his gum into the foaming water.

"You're the one who needs to cool it, Tony," Lila said. Her shapely bottom wiggled in a yellow bikini and her ponytail with its polka dot ribbon shook as she boarded Karen's raft. She looked at Jim to see if he'd noticed.

"Mommy, I'm scared." Artie's wail rose to pierce the serene ambiance as Greg's raft entered the water and headed for some minor rapids.

"It's okay, honey." Rita hugged her son in his bulky life vest and looked at Jim. "I thought you said this kind of rafting wouldn't be dangerous."

"Stop babying Artie, Rita. There's no danger when we have such experienced leaders." He considered his sons to be weaklings who'd been suffocated by their doting mother. When they were little, he had tried to intervene and discipline them. He wanted his boys to play sports and have muscular physiques. But as they shunned physical activities and grew flabby, he had given up. Now, he had to repress urges to berate them.

Conflict over how to rear kids—a topic Jim heard about from his psychiatric patients—had driven him and Rita apart. Off and on Jim had felt cowardly and angry at himself for staying with a wife he no longer respected or loved. But as a child he'd endured his parents' bitter divorce, and memories of their vicious fights still haunted him. He had decided to never subject his own kids to such trauma.

One snowy December night, Jim had met Lila in a cocktail lounge near his office. He would never forget his first sight of her—the hourglass body in a form-fitting, purple sheath, the tumble of blond hair, the exquisite face. He had slid onto a bar stool beside her and gotten lost in her allure.

Early in their affair, Jim had vowed now and then to

give up Lila. He hated sneaking around and lying to Rita concerning his whereabouts. But he'd become addicted to Lila's spontaneity. Her sensuality. Her ability to make him forget the miserable and lonely marriage he would give anything to escape.

Jim knew that having Lila go on his family's rafting trip was risky. But he was too smitten to care. Now, on the river, Jim studied the foamy peaks that danced by flirtatiously. He imagined himself atop one of those peaks, free of his marriage and about to whirl into a whole new start in life with Lila. During their time together, he had become convinced about one thing. He did not want a life without Lila.

Out on the water, the two rafts bobbed up and down under a pure cerulean sky. An eagle performed graceful pirouettes overhead, and a single fisherman was sighted on shore. Otherwise the rafters might have been in their own private cocoon of sun and surf.

"Help!" shouted Isabel. Her summons from Karen's raft shattered the peaceful vignette. "Someone help! Helen's choking on a cough drop."

Tony, seated near Helen, jumped up. He twisted Helen's body sideways, positioned himself behind her, and clasped his arms around her. He started the Heimlich maneuver to dislodge the cough drop. Over and over he exerted pressure on Helen's diaphragm until the drop popped out of her mouth.

"Thank God!" Isabel embraced Helen, who was shaking from the ordeal.

"Yay, my Boy Scout!" Lila gave her son a hug as all the rafters applauded.

Jim, stunned to see a teenager like Tony perform with such expertise, thought of his own sons and how inept they'd be in such a crisis. He felt a crushing sense of failure—as a father and a husband. Only with Lila did he feel like a winner.

That evening, before dinner, the exhausted rafters gathered around another campfire. Karen, who served as the camp chef, was basting chicken with barbecue sauce on a nearby grill. Scented smoke wafted by as the rafters nibbled on cashews and cheese.

After everyone had congratulated Tony one more time for saving Helen's life, Jim swirled pricey Cabernet Sauvignon he'd brought on the trip. He turned to Ryan. "Tell us about yourself. What do you do? Where are you from?"

"Not much to tell really. I'm from Ohio. Business major at Ohio State. Met Shelly there. She's the best thing that ever happened to me." Ryan grinned, creating deep dimples, which made him look like an appealing child.

Jim gazed up at the brilliant North Star and smiled. "Ah, youth. I remember when I dated this college . . . well, you always remember that one special girl, I suppose."

"I'd like to hear more about that girl of yours, Jimmy." Lila's slurred words got partially lost in her laughter.

"Jim!" Rita's summons rose from her nearby tent. "The boys need you. Now."

Lila fixed her gaze on Jim. "One thing I don't under-stand. That wife of yours has a fabulous, handsome hus-band. Me? I'm all alone except for Tony." She flicked ashes off her cigarette. "And I have to tell you, Jimmy, your wife treats you like shit."

"Mom!" Tony choked as he tried to speak with a mouth full of potato chips. "You told me never to say shit. What gives you the right to say it?"

The low hum of other conversations ground to silence. The buzz of insects intersecting in the black sky, and flashes of fireflies with their glowing yellow lanterns, accompanied Jim's finger taps on his wine glass.

Rita rushed up to Lila and leaned close to her face. "I overheard that crack about how I treat my husband, and you calling him Jimmy. Leave him alone."

"Like you do?" Lila's laugh was throaty and mocking.

"Mom. Stop." Tony ground the heel of his tennis shoe into a patch of sand. "You're outta line again."

"Oh, honey boy, ordering his mother how to act." Lila took a sip of wine. "Your daddy, that famous trial attorney, must have taught you to be so feisty."

"No, Mom. You get credit for that."

"Dinner everyone!" Greg clanged a bell with fervor.

"Well, I'm sure as hell not going to eat right now." Lila fingered the linen fabric of a clinging, hot-pink sundress. "I'm going to have another drink." Her eyes canvassed Jim like she was seeking some invisible opening in his pores.

"Rita, you and the other women can go ahead." Jim

gestured to the food where his sons had rushed to be first to eat. As the women lined up, Jim picked up a wine bottle and whispered to Lila, "Let me be a gentleman and pour that for you."

"You're on, Jimmy." Lila giggled and held out her glass.

"Daddy . . . I mean, Dad?" Artie whimpered from the food line. "Where are you?"

"Oh, for God's sake." Jim shook his head in disgust.

As Jim helped Karen flip pancakes the next morning, everyone, except Rita and her sons, chattered with anticipation about rafting and were eager to set off like veteran seafarers. Rita ignored the conversation and hovered over Donny and Artie, who were bickering about who got the maple syrup first.

When they reached the river, Greg launched his daily pre-departure remarks. "Welcome to day two. You've had a full day on the water and should be old pros at braving the rapids. Today will be more adventurous. But you're ready for it."

"I'm scared. I wanta go home." Artie appeared near tears.

"Let's get on with it." Lila flashed a dazzling smile. "My Tony boy here is raring to go, aren't ya, babe?"

Jim raised two fingers in a V-shape. "Atta boy, Tony."

The first hour of rafting was through waters so calm that the river might have been a pond on a windless day.

Into the second hour, some of the passengers were dozing under the bright sun, lulled by gentle waves.

Suddenly, the waters began to churn with a fury, crashing over rocks. A pair of screeching crows swooped overhead as though exhilarated by the turbulent water.

"Do what I told you and you'll be fine," Greg shouted.

Jim clung to his seat as Greg's raft hit the turbulence. "Heigh-ho, Silver!" He felt a sense of excitement that had been absent from his life for years.

Rita grabbed her sons and pushed them to the floor of the raft as they headed into the currents. "Lord Jesus, save us!"

Jim laughed as the waves spilled in and soaked everyone. When the raft veered as if to tip over, he whooped. Not since college, when he courted danger by skydiving, had his heart raced like this. He wanted this feeling of exuberance to continue instead of his sense of suffocation in the morass that his marital life had become.

As the two rafts entered smooth water again, Jim glared at his sons, who hunched together and ducked their heads. When he looked back at the other raft, he saw Tony giving his mother an exuberant high-five.

For lunch on shore, Greg and Karen arranged desserts on a picnic table. As Donny rushed up to grab a chocolate chip cookie, a bee swarmed above it. "Mommy," he yelped.

"What is it, darling?" Rita jumped up from a table

where Jim and Artie were feasting on hot dogs piled with mustard, ketchup, cheese, and pickles.

Lila, seated with Tony at an adjacent table, looked over at Jim. She raised her dark eyebrows and adjusted a strap of her skimpy, black bikini.

Jim slammed a fork on the table and got up. "Rita, I need a word with you. Donny, sit with your brother." Jim motioned Rita to step away from the picnic area.

Rita stared at her husband with accusatory eyes. "You don't have to be so rude to your son, Jim. You'll hurt his feelings."

Jim swallowed hard. "Damn it, Rita. The boys' piss and moan routine has to stop. They're crybabies and wimps who don't have an ounce of manhood in their bloated bodies. You've turned them into sorry-ass mama's boys."

Rita planted both hands on her wide hips. She pointed a sunburned index finger at her husband and hissed, "Maybe if you spent time with them, and me, instead of showing off for sluts like that drunk, Lila, it'd be different."

"Lila has nothing to do with this, though, by the way, her son is masculine and not a fraidy-cat like Donny and Artie."

"There's always a Lila for you to latch onto, isn't there?" Rita stammered. "Don't you think your boys notice that you care more about people like her than them or me?"

Donny rushed to Rita's side and looked at Jim. "Daddy, don't be mean to her."

Jim shuddered and watched Rita retreat with an arm

around Donny. He'd lost the will to fight his wife and her ironclad bond with their sons. Jim felt as he had when his parents battled before their divorce. He was the outsider, helpless to change the outcome.

That night the weary rafting group sipped drinks before dinner. Ryan turned to Jim. "Tonight we get to reverse things and hear about you, Doc. What's it like to be a shrink and listen to all sorts of weirdo problems?"

Behind them the sizzle of steaks on a grill mingled with cricket chirps. Voices around the rafters' circle dwindled to a hush.

"Me?" Jim flashed a crooked grin. "I'm not interesting. Just ask my wife or sons."

Lila juggled a wine glass between her knees and clapped. "Attention, everyone." She cast a radiant smile at Jim and crossed her tanned, bare legs. "We're all sure you are fascinating, Jimmy. So do tell us everything."

"I told you before to quit calling him Jimmy." Rita's face was crimson.

"Sorry. Did we come here to have fun or not?" Lila pouted.

"Okay, briefly, this is all you need to know." Jim launched into a litany of dates documenting high school, medical degrees, marriage, parenthood. He concluded with a wry smile. "I spend most of my time nowadays probing other people's psyches. Sounds pretty dull, doesn't it?"

"But we want to know about the real Jimmy . . . I mean, Jim," Lila said. "What turns you on?" Lila had put on another Technicolor outfit, this one electric-blue shorts and a halter.

Rita pointed at Lila. "Lady, why don't you go suck up to a single guy?"

"Chow time." Greg rang his bell.

After dinner Jim was adjusting a sheet on the mattress when Rita burst into their tent with such force the frame shook. "Jim, what the hell's wrong with you?"

"With me?" Thinking about Lila, Jim's hands caressed the sheet as if it were a newborn.

"That Lila. For God's sake, she's like a prostitute. A lush. A flirt."

"Shut up, Rita. She's a woman alone with her son. That's all. She's harmless."

"You're ruining it, as usual, for the boys and me."

"That's me, Mr. Ruination. Another black mark for Jim." He turned away. "Let's go to sleep. Everything will be better in the morning." As Jim lay on the mattress waiting for Rita to snore, he visualized Lila beneath the seductive full moon, perhaps in her negligee, waiting where they'd agreed to meet. His heart ticked faster than the alarm clock in their tent.

"Jim?" Rita uttered through the thick onset of sleep. "I'm sorry."

Earlier in their marriage, Jim would have appreciated Rita's apology and forgiven her outburst. Now, he felt numb when his wife lashed out at him.

When guttural snores ensured Rita's deep sleep, Jim grabbed a flashlight and stepped outside. The sky was ablaze with glittering stars and flashing meteors. Pebbles crunched underfoot as Jim made his way to a picnic area away from the tents. But no one was there. He was trying to curb his disappointment when Lila crept up behind him, giggled, and tapped his shoulder. "Boo."

Jim turned and grabbed her. His kiss was savage, born of deprivation and longing. His tongue rooted through her mouth as his body shoved up against her.

Lila pulled away and grinned. "Whoa. Jimmy's in need of some TLC. Come to Lila, big boy." She ran a fingernail down his cheek and across his heaving chest.

Jim clung to Lila, raking her back with his fingers and breathing into her ear. "I've been looking for someone like you all my life. Your passion and spirit." He moaned and collapsed against her as she stroked his hair. He laid his head on her shoulder, like a baby being comforted after a crying jag.

"There, there, it's okay. So you've been looking for me, have you?"

"Please, Lila, don't ever leave me. I don't want to live without you."

The next morning was so exquisite that a magic fairy might have created its perfection. Heavy overnight rains left the trees and grass glistening as though they'd been hand-washed. Jim hummed as he tackled a plate of scrambled eggs with bacon and tried to ignore his fighting sons and avoid eye contact with Lila.

"What are you so happy about all of a sudden, Jim?" Despite last night's apology, Rita had notched up her usual morning grumpiness.

"I'm happy that it's such a glorious day." Jim kept his back turned to Rita.

When breakfast was over, Greg clapped his hands. "Let's go." He headed to the water where he ushered everyone onto their rafts. "Today is the big test." He squared his shoulders. "It's our last day of rafting and the Mama Mary Rapids. As I've said, they're categorized as Class III rapids in terms of danger and difficulty. So you can expect medium to high waves. Mama Mary should be bigger and faster than ever after last night's rain. Hang on tight. Do everything we've practiced and everyone will be fine."

"Does someone get a big award for being the bravest today?" Lila grinned at Greg before looking at Jim and winking.

"Lila, you'll get an award just for being one of us." Greg eyed Donny, Artie, and Rita. "Let's all keep working on bravery and good sportsmanship."

As the rafts drifted off, they dipped up and down like pillows atop gentle waves.

"What's so rough about this?" Tony wore a red bandana wrapped around his curly mop of brown hair.

Greg warned, "Pay attention ahead! We're almost at the Mama Mary Rapids. I'll signal when. Stay calm. Enjoy it. I've never lost anyone. And I don't intend to today."

"Bring it on!" Jim raised a clenched fist. His eyes danced like the rippling waves.

"Ride 'em, cowboy!" Lila chimed in.

Just then, Jim spotted the torrent of whitewater ahead. It was whipping and swirling, and making a roaring sound. He felt no fear. Only anticipation.

"Hang on!" Greg yelled before his raft disappeared into the teeming froth.

Donny's "Mommy, we're gonna die!" collided with Tony's "Yahoo" as Karen and her passengers headed into the rapids.

As Greg's raft shot out of the water, Ryan shrieked, "Man, that was awesome."

Adrenalin coursed through Jim as he screamed, "Wow! Amazing! What a ride!" He glanced back to see whether Karen's raft had broken through.

"Good. Here they come." Greg grinned as the second raft appeared.

As her raft emerged, Karen's scream was bloodcurdling. "Greg, Lila's gone!"

Tony kept repeating, "Mom! Where's Mom?"

"Karen, take your raft to shore." Greg's voice quivered. "I'll find Lila."

"I'm going after Mom." Tony jumped into the churning water. As he began dog-paddling back toward the rapids, Jim stood and leaped off Greg's raft. "Wait for me, Tony. I'm coming to help."

Greg grabbed his whistle and blew until his face turned crimson. "Calm down, everyone. Stay in your rafts. Karen and I are taking you to land where you must remain!" He turned toward Tony and Jim, who were swimming away against the current. "Tony! Jim! I'll find Lila. Swim back to shore!"

As both rafts reached the nearby riverbank, Rita stood and flailed her arms toward her husband. "Don't be stupid, Jim. You might die out there."

Once his other passengers were safely on land, Greg headed his raft toward Jim and Tony. Jim's rapid strokes had brought him up to Tony. He'd wrapped one arm around the boy's gyrating torso and was fighting to hold him until Greg arrived.

"Stop!" Tony hit Jim with his free arm. "I have to find Mom. Leave me alone."

When Greg reached the struggling pair, he grabbed Tony's arm and helped him onto the raft. Preoccupied, he didn't notice as Jim twirled around and headed out toward the rapids.

On the riverbank, Rita's pleas for Jim to come back preceded her shriek. "Oh, my God, look!"

A collective scream rose from the rafters at the sight of a body riding the crest of a Mama Mary wave. The body hurtled through the air and landed in a tranquil pocket of water surrounded by jagged rocks. There it floated face-down with a black bikini bottom visible below the orange life vest.

Jim, who'd been about to enter the Mama Mary Rapids, began to swim toward Lila yelling, "Jesus. No! Don't let this be happening." His heart hammered with fear, and he struggled to control his breath.

Greg shouted toward shore, "Karen, call 911."

When Jim arrived at Lila's side, he embraced her neck with one arm. Her mane of blond hair floated about her face like a puffy cloud. With his free hand, Jim flipped Lila onto her back and brushed the hair away from her face. "Don't leave me now that I've finally found you, Lila."

Rita stood with her sons near the water and began to sob. "What the hell are you doing, Jim? Come back!"

On board Greg's raft, Marty was crying, too. Greg patted his shoulder before glancing in Jim's direction. He blanched at the sight.

Jim had brought Lila's lips to his for a passionate kiss. As he treaded water with Lila in his arms, Jim looked toward shore and saw his sons huddled on either side of Rita. He loved them, but in his mind, they belonged to their mother. Not their father.

He did an about-face and began to swim toward the surging rapids with one arm around Lila.

Police sirens screamed as Jim and his silent companion bobbed up and down before disappearing into the Mama Mary Rapids.

A Corvette Cowgirl

Horace pulled the dog treat out of his lunch pail and dangled it before the salivating black Labrador retriever. "Atta boy, Frankie." Horace inserted it in the dog's mouth. "Remember my telling you about planning to have coffee with Joyce from the *Meet-A-Mate* internet dating site?"

Frankie sat perfectly still on the floor of his Humane Society cage and stared intently at the lunch pail as though he could make another treat appear. His concrete-floored cage was large, allowing room for Horace's ample frame.

Horace said to the dog, "So I go to this coffee shop looking for a trim, pretty blonde. Turns out she must have used someone else's photo cuz she was roly-poly and homely." Horace ran a pudgy hand over his thin brown hair and grinned. "But last night I heard from a real looker who seems too good to be true. Calls herself Corvette Cowgirl."

A ringing phone in the front office sent Horace racing out of Frankie's cage past other dogs who erupted with barks and howls. He said to the early morning caller, "We don't open till nine." Horace was not about to explain that, in the five years he'd worked at the Humane Society, he always arrived an hour early to spend time with Frankie. He figured answering phone inquiries for a living didn't mean you had to divulge your daily routine.

Horace had lived in the Upper Midwest, with its wicked winter wind chills and snowbanks, his entire life. An only child, he resided with his widowed, arthritic mother in the 1920s house with a chopped-up floor plan and dated decorating, where he'd grown up. The color scheme was solid beige—draperies, rugs, upholstery.

Beige, with its monotone quality, was how Horace thought of his life. Two decades ago in his mid-twenties, he'd abandoned the goal of living in his own place. After his fiancée Sally passed away, he had given up on the dream of coming home to her, some kids, and a dog in a house they picked out together. He'd adored everything about Sally, who was fun-loving and energetic. Her absence had deprived him of the activities they'd enjoyed together, like comedy movies and going out for ice cream. When Sally died, part of him had, too.

Only recently had Horace begun to consider replacing Sally with someone similarly spirited who could become his wife. Whoever she was would have to love dogs because Horace longed to adopt Frankie more than anything in the world. She'd have to have some money, too, because right now he couldn't afford even a studio apartment on his paltry salary.

Horace had found that the *Meet-A-Mate* site offered an amazing number of women shopping for love. They all boasted about being fit, good-looking, smart, eager, and adventurous. Most hinted about sex but stopped short of specifics.

Besides Joyce, Horace had gotten together with only one other woman. At least Marty had matched her attractive photo. But she seemed to specialize in annoying habits. Giggling constantly. Interrupting every time Horace spoke. Checking her makeup in a compact every few minutes. What computer description could have predicted all that?

Still, Horace remained optimistic about finding the ideal woman.

Last night after dinner, he'd poured Coke in a glass as usual and headed for the basement where he kept a rum bottle behind paint cans. After dumping rum into his Coke, he raced to his computer to see if anyone new had contacted him on *Meet-A-Mate*.

And there she was—the stunning photo of a woman who called herself Corvette Cowgirl. Horace had gasped at her beautiful face. A tumble of blond hair. Dark lashes above blue eyes. A mouth resembling a tidy hair bow. "Five-nine. Built. Fun-loving. Looking for a sensual man," she'd written. Tremors had attacked Horace's body. Visions of Caribbean beaches, string bikinis, and comfy beds had paraded across his imagination.

The next morning as Horace arrived at Frankie's cage, the dog's tail wagged and he yelped with anticipation. Horace stroked his fur, cradled one of his ears, and said, "Kiddo, I don't know what I'd do without you to talk to. Yeah, I know you can't talk back. But I can tell you listen to me."

Frankie pushed his wet nose against Horace's pant leg and eyed the lunch pail.

"How could I forget your surprise?" Horace asked, producing a dog biscuit. He lowered himself to the floor and motioned Frankie to sit beside him. "I need to tell you about this nightmare I had last night. Scared me to death."

It had started as just a dream about his late fiancée, Sally. "She was out riding her bike, smiling and singing like she always did. Then that speeding car hit her," Horace said. Reliving the horrific memories, he began to cry.

Frankie looked at Horace and moaned.

Then, starting with Sally's funeral, the dream had become a nightmare. "I looked in Sally's casket and there was Corvette Cowgirl blinking her eyes at me," Horace said. "Mother showed up and ordered me to stay away from women like Corvette Cowgirl, saying, 'You're better off spending time with all those dogs.' I was so upset that I raced over here to hug you." Horace stroked Frankie's head. "But you weren't here, kiddo. I had lost you, too."

"Horace!" said a loud voice in the hall. "What are you doing in there with Frankie?"

It was Miss Silver, as the Humane Society director insisted everyone address her.

"I heard Frankie whimpering and thought something was wrong," said Horace, getting to his feet. "I'm on the way to my desk."

Horace's job was to provide information about pet adoption, training classes, volunteering, and anything else that came up. He worked surrounded by pet items for sale— dog and cat beds, animal collars, grooming utensils, and pet toys. Horace alternately wore to work his "DOGGONE CUTE" and "CATNIP CRITTERS" T-shirts, which were also for sale.

That afternoon, after finishing his bag lunch and a quick visit to Frankie, Horace returned to his desk and a woman's inquiry on the phone: "My husband wants a Lab. Got any?"

Horace's heartbeats careened. Frankie was the Humane Society's sole Lab. "We have one but he's old and not particularly appealing," Horace said. "If you like big dogs, we have a terrific Irish setter and a beautiful golden retriever."

Silence on the line made Horace hopeful that he had discouraged the caller. He was about to hang up when she said, "We'll come by to see your Lab and the other dogs."

It was Tuesday, the only night each week that Mother left home to attend her bridge club of forty years. Horace relished an uninterrupted evening of courting Corvette Cowgirl via computer and slurping extra glasses of rum with Coke. In the kitchen, there was no sign of dinner preparation. "Mother?" he called, passing through the dining room with its beige tablecloth and matching velvet curtains.

"In here, Horace," Mother called faintly from the plaid living room sofa. "I'm feeling rather poorly," she said as he approached.

Horace wondered whether this was one of her periodic ailments that she used to imply he wasn't paying her enough attention. Next came his resentment. He wanted to be free of her, for good.

In the basement, an email from Corvette Cowgirl made Horace's hands shake. "How about getting together Thursday night?" she proposed.

"Where should we meet?" He pecked away in his two-finger fashion.

"Higginsville," she answered. "Ziggy's Bar, corner of Main & Fourth. Five-thirty."

"Oh, no," Horace muttered. Higginsville was more than two hours away. He'd have to get permission from Miss Silver to take Thursday off. Any encounter with her he dreaded.

"Frankie, I brought you two treats today," Horace said the next morning. "One for today, and one tomorrow cuz I'm not gonna be here." As the dog devoured his biscuits, Horace debated telling Frankie about the phone call asking for a Lab. But the thought of talking about it made him too nervous. So Horace spent their time together describing Corvette Cowgirl.

"I can't believe a woman so gorgeous would want a guy like me," he said. "But maybe, like yours truly, she wants someone reliable to settle down with. I hope she's the one, kiddo, cuz I want a regular life. I'm sick of living with Mother. And I want to adopt you."

Near quitting time, Horace had just requested the next day off work for his Corvette Cowgirl date when an incongruous couple came through the front door. Horace thought the overweight woman looked disheveled and exhausted. Fleshy pockets lay below her flat black eyes. She might have slept in her wrinkled blouse, and a dark stain crossed one tan pant leg.

Her husband was trim and broad-shouldered but his facial features were delicate—pale eyelashes, a slender nose, thin lips. The oddest part was his voice. Its feminine lilt didn't fit with his physique. It was high-pitched with noticeable tremors that lingered like a soprano's falsettos.

"How can I help you?" Horace asked.

"I called about your Lab," the woman said.

"Where is he?" chimed in the man.

"Remember I told you he wouldn't be your best choice," Horace said, scrambling to divert them before going on to rave about the Irish setter and golden retriever.

"We want to see the Lab," the woman insisted loudly just as Miss Silver came in.

"Is there a problem, Horace?" Miss Silver's beady eyes shot from him to the couple.

"The problem is him." The woman pointed at Horace. "He doesn't seem to want us to see your Lab."

"Of course, you can see him. His name is Frankie," Miss Silver said. "Come with me."

Horace began to bite his fingernails. His face felt feverish. He had to stop these people. But by the time he was supposed to leave work, they were still with the dogs and Miss Silver.

By noon Thursday Horace was a nervous wreck about meeting Corvette Cowgirl.

Compounding his jitters was anxiety about the couple who'd come to see Frankie. He could only hope that his disparaging remarks had steered them toward another dog. It was too early in the day for sips of rum to calm him down. Maybe coffee would help.

In a Starbucks bathroom mirror, Horace grimaced at the sight of his terrified face. Apprehensive brown eyes. Beads of sweat on his forehead. Flushed cheeks. And he wasn't even in Higginsville yet. Only the thought of rum in a thermos in his car made him relax a bit. He'd get an early start on the drive and have some along the way.

By the time he neared Higginsville in late afternoon, Horace was enjoying the familiar mellowness that sweet rum ensured. He hoped Corvette Cowgirl would wear something provocative: a tight dress or fluffy sweater. But then a cowgirl might show up in a Stetson and riding boots. He expected her laugh to be throaty and thick with intent.

In Higginsville, Horace followed Main Street, snaking past Woolworths and a root beer stand. Next to Bev's Boutique, he spotted Ziggy's. Its exterior epitomized what he thought of as a joint. Horace figured it was smoky and dim inside. Maybe it'd be so dark that Corvette Cowgirl wouldn't realize he'd subtracted several years off his age in his internet profile. He sucked in his gut, willing the extra pounds he'd also lied about to disappear, and reminded himself she thought his name was George.

He parked across from Ziggy's and scanned the block for a Corvette. None in sight. He adjusted the mirror, sprayed himself with cologne, checked his teeth for food particles, and practiced his most tantalizing smile. "Do it like that," he whispered.

Inside Ziggy's, he squinted through clouds of smoke swirling like tornado funnels. Music throbbed like a migraine headache. He searched for a mane of blond hair. But no one resembling Corvette Cowgirl was perched on a stool. "Rum and Coke," he said, thrusting cash at the bartender. He tried to save a bar seat next to him. But a guy with a Santa Claus build insisted his chunky companion needed to sit down.

Five minutes ticked past the appointed time, then ten. Was it possible he'd mistaken the time or day? Could she have been in a car accident? He cursed himself for not providing Corvette Cowgirl with his cell phone number.

Just then, someone behind him tapped his shoulder. Horace grinned and tried to slow his reaction time. He wanted to remember this moment in a dim sanctuary called Ziggy's when his life changed to the beat of throbbing music. He'd spent so much time lately longing for this moment and relishing its sweetness. Slowly, his smile quivering with anticipation, Horace twirled around on his stool.

"Surprise, George!" said a tremoring voice.

Horace drank in a mass of bleached hair and false eyelashes fluttering above cheekbones slashed with rouge. He blinked hard, trying to adjust to a face that bore no resemblance to its computer photo.

"Georgie, it's okay. I left out one little detail, honey," the blonde said, flipping the mane of hair with a raucous laugh. "I'm really Corvette Cowboy."

Despite being so rattled by this hideous surprise, Horace heard something familiar in Corvette Cowboy's voice. Its timbre was so distinctive and different. Where had he heard that voice? He was not about to stick around for further conversation to find out.

The next morning, Horace's hangover pounded his head. He could hardly remember the long drive home from Ziggy's while cursing Corvette Cowboy all the way. He'd capped off that disastrous rendezvous with more rum and was lucky to have made it back without incident.

Now, his body ached, and all he could think of was telling Frankie about his awful encounter.

On the way to Frankie's cage, Horace had to pass the golden retriever and Irish setter. He prayed one of them would be gone, adopted by the inquiring couple. But each dog barked as he passed. Usually Frankie yipped at the sound of Horace's footsteps. But not today.

Frankie's cage was empty. His dog toys were gone as though the Lab had never lived there.

Horace fought tears and an erratic heartbeat, envisioning Frankie with strangers who didn't know what kind of food he preferred or that he expected a daily treat and cradling of his ears.

Awaiting Miss Silver's arrival so he could inquire about Frankie, Horace paced frantically in front of his cage. When she finally arrived, Horace blurted before Miss Silver could even shake all the snow off her boots, "Who adopted Frankie while I was away?"

"Horace, no need to sound so accusatory," she said sharply. "Do I need to remind you that this organization's mission is to have our animals adopted? Frankie has gone to a new home where I'm sure he will be very happy."

Horace's fierce headache added to his rage. He hated Miss Silver and her snarky personality and imagined his thick fingers at her scrawny neck as he shouted, "Where do the people who took Frankie live?" But reason prevailed. He couldn't afford to get fired.

On Saturdays Horace worked mornings and Miss Silver did not. He'd been awake all night wondering how to access her computer records. She'd always maintained that animal adoption should be as confidential as that of a child. About three a.m. Horace had a breakthrough idea. Humane Society visitors signed a guest log. Hopefully he could track the couple that way.

At work Horace broke into a nervous sweat as he checked last Thursday's visitor names. Luck seemed to be on his side. There was only one couple—Doris and Morrie Sidley from Bellville, a middle-income suburb nearby. Horace found their address easily on Google.

By afternoon the frigid weather had turned unseasonably warm. As Horace's Honda crept past 105 State Street in Bellville, he rolled down his car window. Though the Sidleys' sprawling split-level house was in an expensive neighborhood, it was nondescript with brown shingle siding. The large yard was similarly plain, a few trees and no fenced-in area where Horace had hoped Frankie might be.

Horace was imagining Frankie pacing indoors room-to-room when he heard a moaning bark. It sounded like Frankie but had none of his usual exuberance. Rather, it was mournful and carried a plea to be set free. Horace's heart urged him to knock at the Sidleys' front door. To hell with Miss Silver who might terminate him if she found out he'd violated the rules.

By the time Morrie opened the front door, Horace had decided to tell the Sidleys that the Humane Society routinely inspected pets' adoptive homes.

"Oh, it's you, that guy . . ." Morrie's tremoring voice halted as his eyes widened. He stared at Horace as though he were an alien. Suddenly, Frankie bounded out and yipped with joy. As Horace bent to pet him, the dog licked his face all over. Morrie's face was wet, too, but with perspiration.

While Horace identified himself and began to explain why he'd come, his mind was struggling to place where he'd heard that voice. As Morrie talked again, Horace remembered the setting—a dimly lighted room, loud music, festive partygoers. No! The sweating man standing here in blue jeans in his pricey house couldn't be the same one who . . .

"George? Or is your real name Horace? I bet you recognize my unusual voice, don't you?"

Unable to look Morrie in the eyes, Horace stared at the porch floor and nodded.

"Okay. We need to talk about this situation and figure out a solution before my wife gets home," Morrie said. "She doesn't know about any of this."

On Monday morning Horace arrived at work precisely at nine o'clock. All weekend he'd thought about the proposal Morrie had presented on Saturday. Horace had never considered himself a person who could be bribed, not that anyone had ever tried to coerce him. Yet, here he was on the brink of changing all that.

Miss Silver was already at work and eyed Horace's

puffy eyes. "Wild weekend, or are you coming to work sick?" she needled.

Horace's instinct to throttle his despicable boss was interrupted by Morrie's entrance with Frankie. Once again Morrie had changed personas—first he'd been an audacious dame with a bleached wig, then a weekend guy wearing jeans, and now this man who wore a smart business suit and crisp white shirt.

"Frankie here just isn't working out for us," Morrie told Miss Silver. "I'm returning him."

Horace feigned surprise as Morrie handed over Frankie's leash. As the dog circled his legs in a delirious frenzy, Horace said, "I intend to adopt Frankie."

"Now, wait just a minute." Miss Silver held up a hand.

Morrie said, "With all due respect, Miss Silver, I don't think you value Horace as the exemplary, reliable employee he seems to be."

"But—" she began to sputter.

"No, please let me finish, Miss Silver." Morrie had metamorphosed now into the authoritative executive he role-played on weekdays. "There happens to be a job opening as a teller at my bank. We're looking for someone personable and dependable, just like Horace. So I am inviting him to apply for that position. Today."

Queen For a Day

Dr. Brock Landers thought of Tuesday as D-day, D standing for Doll. It was the day on his weekly psychiatric appointment calendar that brought Martha Matthews, a patient who had no idea the two of them shared the same hobby.

Brock, a strapping one-time California surfer, sported a sun-kissed, light mahogany complexion complemented by a shock of curly gray hair. He exuded a gentleness and sense of calm that soothed patients who were agitated about confiding psychiatric issues. Residents of Brock's oceanside community, near San Francisco, knew him as a do-gooder—homeless meal program volunteer, Chamber of Commerce member, Catholic church greeter. Missing from that roster, though, was the one activity Brock never divulged.

He collected baby dolls.

As a psychiatrist, Brock was aware of the difference between a kinky endeavor and a fulfilling hobby. For him, dolls fit the latter category. But he also knew that a grown man collecting dolls could be considered rather odd. And his wife of thirty-two years, who'd given him three grown daughters, would hardly want to tell their friends, "My husband is into dolls."

He and Laura, his wife, already had other issues to confront. Though their marriage had been happy initially, they had drifted apart the last few years. Once their daughters had left home, Brock realized how little he and Laura had in common. She relished socializing; he did not. She liked modern art; he preferred the old masters. The list of their differences was lengthy. Lately Laura had accused Brock of doting on something other than her, though she was not sure what.

Sometimes he wondered whether he liked dolls so much because they demanded nothing.

On Tuesday at one o'clock, Brock ushered Martha into his modest office. After nearly three decades of counseling patients about lousy marriages, paralyzing phobias, and other afflictions, Brock had established a solid professional reputation. He could afford a swanky office but chose not to advertise his affluence. Instead, he remained in the same drab 1950s-era beige building, and bare-bones office, where he'd started. Other than financing his wife's high-maintenance lifestyle, Brock rarely splurged. Except when it came to his dolls.

As Martha took her usual chair, Brock noticed she'd dressed as if for a cocktail party. A fitted black dress with sheer hose accentuated her long, slim legs. Though a decade older than Brock, who was in his early fifties, Martha was still very attractive with a youthful face, thanks to a facelift. She was also extremely lonely.

Martha supervised an upscale home for the elderly. She had come to Brock several years ago with anger and aggression issues, sent by her husband who'd left her shortly afterward. Ever since, she'd been on the hunt for a male replacement. Considering how flirtatious she was, Brock suspected Martha thought he was a candidate. Once, he'd been almost certain Martha followed him in her car. But when he'd broached the suspicion, she responded with a vehement denial.

Martha was an obsessive collector of ethnic dolls. Each week she brought one carefully wrapped in a large purse. She'd announce their names theatrically as though they were Hollywood stars. Since humor worked best to deflect Martha's attempts to flirt, Brock always began their hour by inquiring about the doll: "Who's your queen for a day this time?"

Today Martha, who had a deep Southern accent, waved a doll arm at Brock and drawled, "Ah-m Lily frahm Korea. We havv a new ray-sah-dent, Say-rah. She braaht a huge dahl cah-llection ah-long."

"You must enjoy looking at them," Brock said.

"Say-rah doesn't need those dahls. Ah-m goin' ta fig-ah out a way ta git them."

Brock watched his patient's eyes turn steely and her

body tense. "As you know, I'll be out of town next Tuesday," Brock said. He did not mention his destination—Paris, which he'd chosen to celebrate Laura's fiftieth birthday and to mend tears in the fabric of their marriage. "While I'm gone, Martha, please don't do anything rash like trying to take Sara's dolls away from her. We'll talk about it two weeks from today when I'm back." He waited for Martha to respond. Her failure to do so made Brock uneasy.

Late Friday afternoon Brock stopped by the single room he'd leased in an office building to store his dolls. Outside, the air was balmy and Brock thought of the nearby ocean. He longed to take a run beside its crashing waves but was due home soon to set up the bar for Laura's dinner party. Entering the building, he thought of how his once-carefree life had turned into one of unrelenting obligations.

Inside, pairs of eyes in sweet baby doll faces greeted Brock. They perched on floor-to-ceiling shelves, arranged perfectly like rows of books. The first doll face Brock always sought was the one he'd named Mimi. Her chubby pink face, framed by gold curls, reminded him of his baby sister, whose name had also been Mimi. When Brock was four, Mimi died unexpectedly.

Afterward, he'd begged his bereft parents for a baby doll to replace his sister.

But his father had stormed, "Boys do not EVER play with dolls."

In medical school Brock had heard students joke about psychiatrists being screwballs who chose that specialty to address their own mental health issues. So he'd considered internal medicine or cardiology but always came back to psychiatry. Analyzing why one person cheated on a spouse or another hid a gambling addiction intrigued him more than diagnosing colitis or operating on a heart. Besides, he'd judged his own mental health to be A-plus, not screwball caliber. Back then, dolls were the last thing on his mind.

Only when his firstborn daughter received a baby doll for Christmas had Brock reverted to his boyhood craving for a doll. His first acquisition had not been planned.

In San Francisco for a medical conference, he'd passed a store window featuring baby dolls. As though propelled by some unseen force, he had gone in. He'd known right away which doll he wanted. She was dressed in a pink, one-piece sleeper outfit with a drawstring at the bottom like his sister had worn. Her eyes were blue and opened or closed like a real baby. There seemed only one appropriate name for her—Mimi.

Back at his San Francisco hotel, Brock had laid the doll on a bed and thought of returning her to the store. What if Laura or someone else found out he'd bought a doll? Yet, just looking at Mimi soothed an aching corner of Brock's heart. He'd decided to keep her for himself a while and eventually give her to his daughter, Melanie.

But Brock had never gotten around to giving Mimi to his daughter.

As his doll collection grew, Brock occasionally thought to himself: *What the hell am I doing?* But then he'd think: *Some guys collect sports paraphernalia, coins, or stamps.* Besides, he didn't play with his dolls or pretend they were real, like Martha did. If dolls brought him joy and some incalculable degree of comfort, his secret hobby wasn't harming anyone, was it?

Now, before leaving his doll storeroom, Brock removed one baby doll from a top shelf. She was wrapped in a yellow blanket with her eyes closed as if sleeping. He put her in a shopping bag and headed for his car.

On Saturdays, Brock served breakfast at St. Xavier's meal program for the homeless. St. Xavier's showed respect for their diners by setting oilcloth-covered tables with real silverware and fake flower centerpieces in a crowded recreation room. By the time Brock arrived, hungry homeless recipients were always lined up for a couple of blocks. As he dished up scrambled eggs and ham slices assembly-line style, Brock tried to greet each person. Some responded. Others refused to make eye contact.

Last Saturday a weary-faced man had stepped up for food holding the hand of a sleepy little girl. Her T-shirt was grimy and her curls tangled. Brock guessed she was three, maybe four.

"No, Daddy," she whimpered as the man tried to hand her a plate.

"Yes, Janie," the father said gruffly.

Brock eyed the father in his threadbare overalls. "If you're here next week, I'll bring Janie a surprise."

Now, a week later, nearly all the food had been served by the time Janie came in with her father. She looked more forlorn than Brock remembered. Janie shuffled in too-large shoes, trying to keep them on. He thought of his own daughters at that age—their shining faces, ironed play clothes, happy smiles. Janie had never experienced any of what his girls took for granted.

Once Janie and her father were seated, Brock delivered the shopping bag with the doll.

As he began to say Janie should wait till they left to open it, she pulled out the doll and squealed.

Another little girl nearby said, "Where'd you get that?"

"Him." Janie pointed at Brock.

"Can I have one, too?" asked the second girl.

"Sure, honey. Next time," Brock said.

On the plane to Paris, Brock and Laura toasted her birthday with champagne in their business class seats. As Laura prattled on about the jam-packed itinerary she'd planned, Brock dozed and dreamt. First, Martha paraded past clutching a pile of dolls. Next came Janie, who stretched out her arms for a plate of food. Then he was in his doll storeroom looking at Mimi on a shelf when Laura nudged him to wake up.

"You were saying, 'Mimi, Mimi!'" Laura said. "After all these years, are you still dreaming about your sister?"

"Once in a while."

After arriving at DeGaulle airport, Brock and Laura took a cab to their hotel. Brock had first visited Paris as a student on a shoestring budget. Its sights had enchanted him—the graceful Seine River, lively sidewalk cafes, grandiose architecture, lovers on nearly every corner. None of that had changed, at least from the taxi window.

Laura, who was svelte and stylish and had a clothes-horse reputation among her socialite friends, had designated several hours to shop alone in Paris. Such outings bored Brock. So the day of her shopping spree, he perused tourist brochures in the hotel lobby. It was an exquisite, crisp autumn afternoon and he'd almost settled on walking through Montmartre when an ad for La Musee de la Poupee (The Museum of the Doll) caught his eye. He'd never heard of it. But since it was near the Pompidou museum, he could tell Laura he'd gone there.

On the outside, the doll museum was unpretentious with a charming small courtyard and was adjacent to a park called Jardin Anne Frank. Inside were four rooms jammed with more than five hundred dolls, mostly French dating from 1800 to the 1950s. Wandering by their showcases, Brock was struck by their outfits, which reflected various periods of history. He stopped at a display of baby dolls and thought how much Martha would relish all this.

When he spotted a doll that looked a lot like his sister

Mimi, Brock's mind strayed to the day she had disappeared. At least, that was how it'd seemed to him as a four-year-old.

Mimi had been wailing in her upstairs crib. Before their mother rushed into the baby's room, Brock had pulled a chair to the side of the crib and climbed up. He'd reached down to pat Mimi's velvety skin, which was bright red from crying. She was gagging, and Brock worried she'd stop breathing any minute. He'd patted her some more but she cried even louder.

When his mother arrived, she'd scolded Brock for being up on the chair. "Get down right now," she'd ordered before picking up Mimi and racing out. Brock had obeyed, wondering whether he'd done something bad to make his little sister cry so hard.

The days that followed had been chaotic—his parents leaving him with a sitter to be with Mimi in the hospital. Then one day, they'd come home ashen-faced. Mimi had gone to Heaven to be with Jesus, they told Brock. After that no one explained who or what caused Mimi to die.

Brock had been too afraid to ask his parents whether something he'd done contributed to her death. He'd worried that maybe his fingers were dirty and Mimi got their germs. Or had he patted Mimi too hard and hurt her? Exaggerated fears of a four-year-old took root and dominated Brock's boyhood. Later, as an adult, he understood that Mimi's death was not his fault. But like many childhood phobias, unrealistic traces of guilt still lingered.

Before leaving the doll museum, Brock stepped into

its gift shop, which sold dolls and accessories. One shelf held a baby doll unlike any in his collection. She had the sweetest face Brock had ever seen and long eyelashes that looked genuine. Before he knew it, Brock was handing euros to the clerk in exchange for the doll. He had worn a backpack and intended to hide his new purchase inside it.

Out on the sidewalk, about to stash away the doll, he heard, "Brock? What on earth are you doing here?" It was Laura, who rushed up and stared at the doll dangling in his hand.

"I might ask you the same question," Brock said.

"You know how much I love modern art so I'm on my way to the Pompidou museum."

Laura glanced at the sign advertising the doll museum. "Poupee means doll, right?" Her eyes narrowed. "Is that where this doll came from?"

"I got it for one of my patients."

"Since when are you a child psychiatrist?"

Brock looked at his wife and thought: *Here we are in romantic Paris and Laura is already needling me. And wouldn't you know she'd catch me with a doll.* He decided to ignore her jab. "How was your shopping?"

"Great. I left all the damage I did at the hotel." She frowned. "Did you come to this part of Paris just for that museum? Otherwise, what are you doing here with a doll?"

"Laura, did I ask what stores you went to and what you bought? No. I'm really tired of you second-guessing everything I do." He put an arm around her shoulder. "Now, let's enjoy, as they say, gay Par-ee."

Laura flashed that look Brock knew so well. It meant that his wife would catalog this event and parade it out later for further examination.

As the plane touched down in California, Brock phoned his office for messages.

Bonnie, his receptionist, said, "I guess you haven't heard."

"Heard what?"

"About your patient, Martha Matthews. Yesterday's newspaper said she's been accused of stealing from someone in her elder care place. You won't believe what she stole—some doll collection worth several thousand dollars."

Brock feigned disbelief at the news about Martha. But he wasn't surprised. The glint in his patient's eyes that last visit had warned him she intended to get her hands on Sara's dolls.

Mostly, Brock was worried about his own liability if Martha were charged with elder abuse due to criminal theft over a certain monetary sum. Under California law, he was obligated to cooperate with an investigation if he knew of such abuse. Then he'd be drawn smack-dab into the doll theft issue. And what if the authorities somehow found out that he, a respected psychiatrist, was a furtive collector of dolls?

"Did the article say anything about Martha being arrested?" Brock asked Bonnie.

"No, just accused. She hasn't cancelled her appointment with you next Tuesday."

On Tuesday Martha appeared wearing an expensive, gray wool dress with chunky jewelry. She looked remarkably calm for someone charged with theft and abuse. She pulled a statuesque doll in a dance costume from her purse and drawled dramatically, "She's Sahn-ya fra-hm Aar-gan-tina. This queen fah a day does th-ah taan-go."

Brock thought better of asking whether Sonya was from Martha's own collection or the one stolen from Sara. "Martha, I understand there's a problem with you and the doll collection belonging to your resident, Sara. We need to talk—"

"Oh, thaat. Say-rah's fah-mily's out to cause trouble. I ah-m no thief."

"But did you physically take Sara's dolls away from her?"

"Ah jest bah-rowed thaam for a while."

And so it went for the next hour as Brock tried to substantiate whether Martha had committed elder abuse. By the end of their session, it had become clear that she was guilty.

At dinner that night, Laura and Brock sat at opposite ends of the lengthy table in their formal dining room.

Laura loved this room with its silver service on a buffet and cut-glass chandelier, while Brock preferred a casual meal in the kitchen. To him, the stately Mediterranean-style spread Laura had insisted they needed was far too large and grandiose.

Laura ran a manicured nail through her streaked, blond pageboy. "I invited the Blairs for cocktails this Saturday."

Brock finished a bite of chicken. "He's a bore."

"You're such a grouch lately," Laura said. "You never used to be so negative. Even in Paris you seemed different, preoccupied with little interest in me."

"Sorry. Just a lot on my mind." He folded his linen napkin.

"No, Brock, I know it's something else. I never thought I'd have to ask you this." Laura's voice trembled. "Are you involved with someone else?"

Brock fixed a penetrating stare on his wife. "Come on, Laura. You must be joking." He angled for humor. "Watching too many soap operas lately?"

"Well, something's wrong. You're not yourself." She stood and picked up her plate.

Early Saturday morning Brock stopped by his storeroom to choose a doll for the homeless child who'd asked for one. In the past, a sense of calm had overtaken him while gazing at his dolls' innocent faces. Over the years, Brock had rarely picked up a doll just to hold it. Looking at them had always sufficed.

                    Detours

But today Brock felt agitated. Though he hated to admit it, Laura had been right in saying he was not acting normally. Resorting to humor, he thought: *Dr. Landers, maybe you're the one who needs a psychiatrist.*

At the homeless program, Brock gave the little girl his doll and asked her to wait until later to look at it. But no sooner had he turned his back than she was exclaiming with delight, attracting the attention of another child who wanted one, too.

Before heading home Brock answered a phone message from his weekend answering service. Apparently the authorities investigating Martha's elder abuse case had learned she was being treated by Brock. They'd called, left a phone number, and wanted to hear from Brock on Monday.

As a boy, Brock's neighborhood gang had played a Western game. One pretended to be a cowboy and the others tried to lasso him with a rope. Once, a kid had gotten carried away and tightened Brock's lasso to the point he felt breathless and scared. Now, Brock had a similar sensation. It was as if the looming abuse investigation, his wife's suspicions, and the secret doll collection had converged to squeeze him to death.

Over cocktails at home, Brock found Art Blair as boring as ever. He was an engineer and seemed obliged to provide exhaustive details about any subject. As he droned on, Brock's mind drifted to his looming conversation with the abuse authorities. How deeply would they probe, and what would they want to know about him?

As Laura asked Art a question, Brock made his decision. Somehow he needed to hide his doll collection in a completely secret place. Before Monday.

"Brock?" Laura's voice cut through his churning thoughts.

"Must say you look rather worried, old boy," said Art.

"See, Brock?" Laura said. "Other people are noticing something's wrong with you."

After ushering at Sunday church, Brock told Laura he had errands to run.

"What errands?" she asked.

"Our anniversary is coming up," he said. "I'm going shopping."

"In thirty-two years, you've never shopped for our anniversary."

"People can change," said Brock. Overnight he'd come up with a plan to vacate the doll storeroom. There was a locked closet in his medical office that might accommodate all the dolls if he crammed them in vertical stacks. And he had the only closet key.

Now, on a third trip from the storeroom to his office, Brock was exhausted. He was halfway through piling up dolls when he heard footsteps in his office waiting room. In his haste, he must have forgotten to lock the building's front door.

"Aaa-r ya in thaar, Dr. Land-ars?"

Brock froze. What the hell was Martha doing here? It was too late to lock his office door. He could hide in the closet. But how would he explain the dolls stacked everywhere? As his office door swung open, he said, "Martha, you cannot barge into my office like—"

Martha was speechless at the sight of dolls littering the room where she'd spent so many hours as a patient. She was wearing a short skirt with a clinging jersey top and rhinestone belt. Her mascara and lipstick were thick. Her appearance suggested an intended seduction.

"So, ya are a dahl cah-llector like me." Martha winked at Brock. "Your lil secret?"

"I don't know why you're here, Martha, but you need to leave."

She moved toward him, teetering on perilously-high heels as footsteps sounded in Brock's waiting room.

Suddenly, Laura was in his office. "Brock, you ARE with another woman!" Her eyes swept across the piles of dolls. "What on earth are all these—?"

"Looks ta me like he's a clah-set case dahl cah-llector." Martha sneered. "So now I cahn tell those abuse folks thay can't bah-lieve anything Dr. Land-ars says about me cuz he is naht a truth-fahl person. Otherwise he would havv admitted he cah-llects dahls."

"Martha, you can tell them anything you want," Brock said. "By that time I won't have these dolls because I'm giving them all away to homeless little girls."

"Brock, none of this makes sense—this woman, all

these dolls, your weird behavior," said Laura. "We really need to talk."

"Yes, Laura, we do." He held out a couple of baby dolls. "There are things I need to tell you about these, and especially about Mimi."

JUNGLE FEVER

The Boa constrictor's undulation reminded Roscoe of ocean waves he'd watched on a TV travel show. Like those foamy gyrations, the snake writhed inside his cage at the zoo with effortless grace. A spotlight shone down on the snake's arrow-shaped head with its brown stripes on a cream background. Slowly the Boa maneuvered its thick girth onto a large piece of wood surrounded by vegetation. Coiled and motionless, the snake evoked some exotic prehistoric specimen.

Roscoe pressed his bald head close to the cage's glass, hoping to hear the creature hiss. Without warning, the snake came to life and crashed against the window. Roscoe jerked away as a tongue, thin as a needle, burst from the Boa's mouth. Perspiration poured down Roscoe's jowly face and onto his shabby work shirt, and his dark eyes glittered like the beast staring back at him.

"Hey you, Big Boy," Roscoe yelled. "Don't think you can scare me." He shoved shaking hands into the pockets of his baggy overalls. "Didn't bring you a rat today but somebody'll feed you one soon. You know, I've been thinking about trying to get you out of this joint. Now, I'm wondering whether this here zoo might be the best place for you if you're gonna act real crazy like that."

At home in his studio apartment, Roscoe hunkered into the battered cushions of his sofa and took a long sip of cold beer. He contemplated a caramel-colored living room wall. He hated the color, just like he detested caramel candy. His thoughts turned to Big Boy and he muttered, "Geez." He said it softly at first, then louder. "GEEZ."

Whenever Roscoe uttered that "G-word," as his high school pals had dubbed it, he visualized their science teacher, the man they'd nicknamed Bug Beater Seymour because he idolized bugs. When Roscoe or his friends had mentioned the G-word, Bug Beater said, "No slang in this here school."

Bug Beater had loved all animal life, especially skittish lab rats or croaking frogs about to be dissected. But he'd been rhapsodic about only one creature. "BOW-UH CON-STRICT-UR," he'd say before making the proclamation: "Boys and girls, this mighty specimen is the undisputed king of the jungle."

Staring at his caramel living room wall and hearing Bug Beater Seymour wax on about Boa constrictors, Roscoe thought he heard a hiss. Then he saw a razor-sharp tongue vibrate ahead of a fat reptile body as it danced across the wall. "What the heck are you doing here, Big Boy?" he said to the imaginary wall image. "Make yourself at home." Roscoe uncurled himself from the sofa and headed to the refrigerator for another beer.

That night at work, Roscoe checked a clock on the factory wall. Its hands seemed to have stopped moving. He had come to despise the night shift, especially the last couple of hours as they inched toward seven in the morning. He figured a moron could do his job of attaching four bolts per lawn mower as each one reached him on the conveyor belt. Yet, graveyard shift pay was better than daytime work. And he could pay off Sylvia faster with the extra money. But no one had warned him that the skeleton crew slaving on the nighttime assembly line was as weird as Sylvia, the wife he'd finally ditched.

Among the weirdos at work was harelipped Henry, who wore a permanent scowl and ate rotten-looking bologna sandwiches piled with pickles. The guy nicknamed Tiny was at least friendly, though Roscoe got sick of watching him spit snuff in corners near the assembly line. Lars, with his thick Russian accent, was impossible to understand. That left Ralphie, the only one who seemed normal to Roscoe. Ralphie was divorced, too, and always on the prowl.

Roscoe had toyed with the notion of skipping work tonight. Then he'd realized his paycheck would be waiting at the cubicle window when he left work at dawn. How could he have forgotten that when Sylvia kept bombarding him with nasty phone calls about delinquent alimony? He asked himself almost daily what point there was in working at all. The money was turned over to Sylvia before he ever got his hands on it. Somehow he needed to delete his ex-wife from his life.

Most mornings, after a couple of post-work beers with Tiny and Ralphie, Roscoe headed home to catch some sleep on his lumpy mattress. Lately the booze seemed to wake him up instead of acting like a sleeping pill. He'd toss and turn, thinking about ways to drop out of his dismal world. Roscoe figured wherever he headed to escape, it had to be a place his vicious ex-spouse couldn't find him. He remembered a movie about a disgruntled guy who decided to chuck it all. Spur-of-the-moment the fellow threw clothes in a grocery bag, gulped the last soda in his refrigerator, turned off his answering machine, tore up his overdue bills, tucked his ugly little dog under one arm, and walked out of his flat for good.

Roscoe always stopped replaying that film in his mind when he got to the part about the dog. It wasn't that he wanted one himself. He'd despised dogs ever since a German shepherd nearly bit off his nose when he was a kid. Yet, running away with someone, a dog or even a snake, might be more fun than doing it alone. The movie never explained where the man went.

Roscoe figured it was another country, someplace cheap like Mexico. But Roscoe had no intention of going south of the border. He couldn't speak Spanish. And the thought of tacos, with all that spicy sauce, made him feel queasy. He pictured some dark, secret hideout kind of place with no phones jangling or radios blaring depressing news. Maybe it should be somewhere like the jungle.

A few weeks ago, someone at the zoo had tacked up "REPTILE HABITAT" jungle posters near Big Boy's cage. They didn't say what country you had to go to for the dense greenery pictured on them. Wherever it was, Roscoe felt certain that plenty of Big Boy snakes must live there. Lingering in front of the posters, he'd shivered with excitement just thinking about such a spot. Big Boy would probably be a lot happier living in the jungle instead of that cramped zoo cage. There was no way to ask him how he felt about it, of course.

Roscoe imagined the jungle was chock-full of wildlife, just like the zoo's gift shop windows. Behind glass, stuffed monkeys dangled from fake tree limbs, Technicolor parrots were suspended in the air, and fat rubber snakes were positioned on the dirt floor.

Inside the shop, monkey screeches and bird calls competed for the shoppers' attention. Whenever Roscoe had a spare couple of bucks, he stopped at the shop and bought a rubber Boa. He had draped them over furniture and tabletops in his apartment so he'd always have a Boa nearby.

One morning after work, Roscoe was trying to catch a nap when he heard his front door open and a voice call, "ROSS-COE?" How the hell had Sylvia gotten in, he wondered, as the strident tone of his ex-wife assaulted him. It catapulted him back to a marital state of despair and rage. Her screech reminded him of the zoo's gift shop monkey calls. He must have forgotten to lock his apartment door.

"Listen to me, Roscoe. You owe me money," Sylvia shouted as she came in. Her chewing gum crackled in concert with her voice.

Roscoe didn't have to look at Sylvia to imagine her towering in high heels. Her hands would be planted on broad hips and her red mouth twisted in a sneer. He smelled sickening perfume emanating from her rather than the usual cigarette smoke. Oddly he felt curious about what getup Sylvia might have chosen to wear for this unexpected visit.

Roscoe turned toward her in slow motion and inventoried the woman who had once enraptured him. The ankles he used to tickle in hopes of making her giggle. The thick knees every woman in her family had inherited. His eyes had reached her waist, where some bauble hung from a belt, when she noticed a rubber Boa on the back of a chair.

Sylvia bellowed, "Have you forgotten that I'm scared to death of snakes?"

"Okay, so then leave." He retrieved the rubber snake and jiggled it in the air.

"Let go of that snake! Have you lost your mind?"

She glanced around at all the other fake Boas. "You're impossible, Roscoe. Marrying you was the worst mistake I ever made." Sylvia narrowed her eyes. "I want my money right now."

"Silly Sylvie." Roscoe clicked his tongue before sticking it out at her.

"Don't use that nickname. I hate when you do that."

"Silly." Her whack across his left ear set off whirring noises.

Roscoe's meaty hands tightened around the rubber snake's neck. "Sssss," he whispered, lifting it and pushing its head against her leg.

"Die, Roscoe," Sylvia screamed. "You deserve to die." She stormed off.

As Roscoe watched her depart, fragments of their once-sweet marital dreams got tangled up with sour memories.

"Die yourself," he whispered, cradling his snake. "Big Boy, it's time for Sylvia to do just that."

That night at work, over the whirr of factory machines, Roscoe heard Ralphie yell, "Watch it, Roscoe! Nearly missed a mower going by. You'll get docked for that."

"Huh?" Roscoe swiveled to look at Ralphie through his thick safety eyeglasses.

"Thanks, pal. Guess I gotta stop having those daydreams."

"Dreams about broads, right?" Ralphie thumped Roscoe on the shoulder of his soiled denim shirt. "About 'em wearin' next to nothin', like sassy Susanna up there?" He glanced at a provocative female posed on a swimsuit calendar taped to the factory wall.

"Yeah, right," Roscoe shot back. All he could think of was whether Big Boy would prefer to be set loose in Sylvia's house or her car. Would he like sliding across her hideous green shag bedroom carpet or navigating those awful fur-covered seats some car salesman had talked her into? Big Boy looked more like the carpet type, Roscoe decided. If the Boa headed the right direction once inside Sylvia's house, he could rock-and-roll his way right into her bedroom.

While Ralphie prattled on about broads, Roscoe relived yesterday's zoo visit with Big Boy. He was convinced the snake had started to recognize him and welcomed his companionship. Why else would Big Boy move close to the cage's glass when Roscoe arrived?

"Hey, Big Boy. You're looking good, all happy to see me," Roscoe had murmured to the snake. "About ready for our road trip together, big fella?"

The snake had flicked its tongue and arched its back as if in response.

"Yes? Is that what you're saying?" Roscoe had studied the glass enclosure, which was sealed as tightly as a lasso around a calf's neck. "You wanta come along with me, I know. But how the devil am I gonna get you out?"

A couple of nights later, hours were dragging by at work when Ralphie snapped his fingers in Roscoe's face. "Earth to Roscoe. Thinking broads again?"

"Nope. And can you cut that kinda talk?" Roscoe offered a weak laugh to let Ralphie know he was half-kidding. "I got enough grief with Sylvia to never want another broad, well, at least for now."

"Get yourself a cat or dog. Or how about a bird that don't talk?"

"Got my eye on something else," Roscoe said.

"Like a turtle?" Ralphie laughed so fiercely that he nearly choked.

Roscoe lowered his voice. "Boa, Ralphie. A blessed Boa constrictor."

"A SNAKE?" Ralphie's eyes widened. "You're joking."

"Shh. It's just between you and me," Roscoe said.

Ralphie whispered, "Ain't gonna believe this but I know someone else who's goofy for Boas. Poor guy's gotta sell his cuz he can't afford all the rats they eat."

"Yeah?" Roscoe's heart crashed like the metal parts clanking along the conveyor.

"Durn, all you screwballs wanting snakes instead of broads," Ralphie said.

"We're just strange, I guess, your snake guy and me." Roscoe snorted. "I might be interested in talking to him. Got his phone number?"

Late the next morning, Roscoe stood before the snake's cage swaying from one more after-work beer than he usually drank. "Big Boy, I'm real sorry," he said. "There's no way I can get you out from behind that glass. Don't get jealous or nothing, pal. But I found one of your brothers who needs adopting." He waved goodbye to the snake. "Stay safe, big fella. I'm gonna miss you."

That afternoon Roscoe purchased his Boa. It left him with a total net worth of one ten-dollar bill, assorted coins, and a metal carrying case containing his treasure. Ralphie's friend Danny, who sold him the seven-foot Boa named Buster, had issued a list of instructions. Talk quietly to Buster. Let him wander around your house. Feed him one large rat per week. Roscoe wasn't about to tell Danny that he wasn't going to keep Buster, and couldn't have afforded the rats anyway.

As he deposited the snake case on his car's back seat, Roscoe said, "You may be used to being called Buster the Boa, big fella. But I'm going to call you Bigger Boy. You're as heavy as a pile of gold bricks."

As the snake thrashed about, Roscoe squared his shoulders and said, "Geez, Bug Beater Seymour should see me now."

Roscoe parked a block away from Sylvia's house. The snake case was so heavy that Roscoe wasn't sure he could make it a block. Midway, he had to stop to rest on a bench. People passing by looked curiously at the metal case since banging noises were coming from inside. They also stared at Roscoe whose shirt and face were drenched with sweat on a cool fall day.

Sitting there, Roscoe thought about releasing Bigger Boy. Danny had shoved the snake head first into the case. "Wouldn't wanta lose a finger to Buster," he'd cracked. Since reaching in to get the snake wouldn't work, Roscoe decided to open the case's door and let Bigger Boy make his own exit. He savored the possible refrains of Sylvia's inevitable squeals at the sight of the Boa.

Sylvia was apt to scream, "Lord help me!" or "Don't let me die!" He imagined his ex-wife's terrified eyes and quivering mouth as the snake slithered toward her. Perhaps she would be stepping out of the shower and dabbing herself with one of those red towels he'd always detested. Or she might be on the telephone yapping away in her mindless prattle with her back turned to Bigger Boy. Then again she might be standing frozen in terror while the Boa coiled himself around one of her ankles to cut off circulation.

By the time Roscoe reached Sylvia's house, he had lost feeling in his right arm from hauling the snake. Sylvia's car was not out front so he mounted the porch steps and tried the handle. When it turned, he muttered, "Thank you, Silly Sylvie," to a woman who still left her door unlocked as he'd instructed her not to so many times.

In Sylvia's entry hall, with its gaudy floral wallpaper, Roscoe put the case on the floor. The house was silent but for the ticking grandfather clock. He was about to release

Bigger Boy when remorse swept over him. He wanted the Boa for himself, to cuddle with him on the sofa or to watch him maneuver across the floor. He'd already given Sylvia nearly all his money. Why should she get the most important thing in his life?

As he stood there debating, Roscoe heard Sylvia in the adjacent bedroom say, "Darling? How's my sweetie? I'm counting the hours till we're together. You're the dearest man who ever lived. I love you."

Hatred suffused Roscoe. He opened the bedroom door just enough so that he could put Bigger Boy's case on the carpet. Luckily Sylvia, who was still talking on the phone, was facing the window with her back to the door. Roscoe opened the case, shut the bedroom door, and whispered, "Go get Sylvia and kiss her for me where it hurts, Bigger Boy."

Roscoe felt giddy as he raced down the street to his car. He'd nearly reached it when a woman on the sidewalk, with a poodle at her side, shouted, "Watch where you're going. You almost stepped on my darling Reginald."

"Up yours, lady." Roscoe spit toward her. "Same goes for your dog."

Roscoe began to run, stumbled, hit his head on the curb, and fell face up into the street.

"Stupid old woman," he muttered. "Bigger Boy should go after you and that ugly poodle of yours when he's done with Silly Sylvie."

Roscoe lay on the concrete and gazed up at the sky.

Voices jangled above. Hands touched him. But he was concentrating on a slash of sun that had broken through the cloud cover. It was transforming the sky to a medley of lavender, peach, and rose. Its fingers of color transported him past the clouds and deposited him in a jungle, where shards of filtered light cast shadows that danced like ghosts. Someone was trying to lift him from the concrete. But all Roscoe wanted to do was lie on his jungle floor. He closed his eyes in exhaustion. Overhead, screeching birds competed with the peal of ambulance sirens. Roscoe imagined that he heard a hiss nearby. He tried to open his eyes but failed.

A man's voice commanded, "Stand back!"

Roscoe thought he heard something hiss again. He struggled to speak. "Tell me that you got Sylvia, Bigger Boy."

He opened his eyes in time to see a whirling canopy of red lights. The birds' songs had become blaring sirens. "Bigger Boy, wait for me. I'm coming," Roscoe whispered. He imagined Bigger Boy moving by with Sylvia's foot in his mouth. The snake dipped its head as if beckoning Roscoe to follow him further into the murky jungle.

Numero Uno

Lily Chambers thought of her mind as an artist's canvas on which she'd once painted Technicolor flowers. Lately her mental canvas was often blank and she couldn't remember how to draw tulips or daisies. Then abruptly her memory would surge forth, as it did now.

"Doctor Ames is wrong. I do remember things," Lily insisted to her husband, Paul. "I don't belong here in this stupid memory unit."

"What day of the week is it, Lily?" Paul quizzed from a rocking chair beneath his wife's framed oil painting of yellow sunflowers.

Lily searched the somber face of a man with features as familiar as those of her three sons. "Sunday?" She giggled nervously, acting like a naughty child expecting to be scolded.

"Lily, it's Tuesday. While you're awake, I need to tell you about your Numero Uno."

Lily had nicknamed Victor, her oldest son, Numero Uno. She stared at her husband of four decades and felt uneasy about Victor. She thought the drawn expression on Paul's face telegraphed bad news. She agonized, too, about her unreliable memory. Had she really fast-forwarded two days? Or was Paul trying to convince her she belonged here and was losing her mind?

Lily closed her eyes and pretended to sleep. She needed to make a plan to escape this square box of a room, which she despised, and could think of only one person daring enough to rescue her. But the man's name, which once dominated her daily thoughts, had evaporated like morning dew on a rose garden beneath sunshine. His was a name Paul had made her promise years before never to utter again. Somehow she needed to remember it, then contact him.

On Wednesday morning Paul entered Lily's room at his usual ten o'clock. His down jacket was damp from snowflakes cascading out of a gloomy Midwestern sky.

During Lily's two months here, Paul had established an unvarying routine to tidy her bare-bones room— adjusting the window shade to mid-height, straightening the comforter, wiping a bedside table with his linen handkerchief. To make Lily's room feel more like their cozy Cape Cod home, Paul had brought her rocking chair, two of her paintings, and her favorite throw pillows. Still, nothing could erase the institutional presence of medicine bottles and uniformed nurses.

Lily had always found Paul's penchant for neatness, perfected during his Air Force career, a reassuring antidote to her own messiness. As he fussed with the room's details, Lily kept her eyes closed. She figured Paul was going to urge her again to participate in a group activity, like cooking or sewing. She was sick of Paul and the doctor chiding her for not being more active. All she wanted was to get out of here, away from all these strangers.

Lily heard Nancy's brisk footsteps cross the wood floor as the nurse said, "Mr. Chambers, good morning." Lily considered Nancy, plump and good-humored, the facility's sole upbeat employee. Nancy spewed jokes as if they would cure a patient's ills.

"Lily had a bad day yesterday, Nancy." Paul sighed. "She didn't know it was Tuesday."

Lily detected a despairing edge in Paul's voice, the sign he'd lost patience with her.

Nancy joshed, "Wish I could lose a couple days away from my bratty sixteen-year-old. I'd like to lock him in a closet."

Nancy motioned Paul to step out in the hall to talk.

Outside Lily's room Nancy said, "I've been trying to get Mrs. Lily interested in doing a memory box to remind her of the past. No luck."

"I remember Doctor Ames describing that as a box of personal mementoes like photos, wedding, or vacation souvenirs, that sort of thing," Paul said.

"Mrs. Lily doesn't want to do anything. Yesterday I

convinced her to eat breakfast in the dining room. It was a disaster. She refused to talk to anyone."

Paul shook his head. "I wish you'd known the old social Lily. Everyone considered her a party girl. She was always laughing, flipping her long curly hair about, flirting with her pale blue eyes. She was so sunny and happy, even silly sometimes."

"I get occasional glimpses of that personality," Nancy said. "Have you told her about Victor? Saturday will be here soon."

"I tried once, but she dozed off before I could tell her." Paul's voice cracked with emotion. "I'll try to tell her again today. It's getting urgent."

When Paul and Nancy returned to Lily's room, she appeared to be asleep. Paul said in a low voice, "Our middle son Danny is coming from LA this afternoon. Nick, the youngest, will be here soon, too. Victor was Lily's favorite son. I'm afraid telling her about him will destroy what's left of her memory."

At the mention of Victor, Lily tried to concentrate on him. She had just conjured an image of Victor in his baby stroller when the shut-off valve of her mind kicked in, sending her to that empty space once chock-full of memory.

After lunch—eaten from a tray—Lily was dozing in her rocking chair when she heard the raspy voice of her son Danny. "Greetings, Colonel!"

Paul's baritone boomed, "How often have I asked you not to call me Colonel?"

Lily opened her eyes and stared at her son, thinking life in California had made him more flamboyant than ever. His bright orange T-shirt, embossed with a dragon, clashed with a wild peroxide haircut. A shiny silver earring decorated one earlobe. Rows of intricate tattoos paraded down both arms. Lily did not have to look at her husband to know he was horrified. Danny, slim and vibrating with energy, had delighted in shocking his father since childhood. He especially relished ribbing Paul about being an Air Force colonel.

Lily remembered Danny as a toddler who, even then, had been a whirling dervish. He'd been the complete opposite of his timid brother, Nick. Now, she heard Danny spew accusations.

"Colonel, this place is lousy. Crackerbox room. One tiny window. That antiseptic smell."

"Do you think I wanted to bring your mother here?" Paul's whispered tone reflected his angst. "I couldn't take care of her myself. You'll see that she can seem normal, then drift off and go blank. Sometimes she hallucinates. Last week, she insisted someone was stealing from her room. Mostly, all she wants to do is sleep."

So this was how it felt to be invisible, Lily thought. *People discussed you as if you weren't there. How dare Paul portray her as mindless? Just because she forgot things didn't mean he should get to decide everything.* She admired his decisiveness but not his need for control.

"Colonel, I'm not dead yet!" Lily fluttered her eye-lashes and made a cackling noise.

"Good for you, Mom!" Danny clapped his hands. "See, Colonel, Mom's still got her old go-get 'em spirit."

Paul frowned. "She's putting on an act for you, Danny. Go back to sleep, Lily."

After Lily feigned sleep, Danny blurted, "Where did Victor's plane crash?"

"Shh, Danny. Your mother might be listening."

"Looks like she's totally gone, Colonel. So what did the Air Force people tell you?"

"Victor was testing a newly designed airplane in Nevada. They're sure the accident wasn't his error since he was such a proficient pilot."

Lily entertained a vision of Victor, a confident and cocky pilot, towering in resplendent Air Force blues. Then along came a different pilot, the one whose name she couldn't recall. The two airmen marched side-by-side, their chiseled faces and lean frames nearly carbon copies.

Lily called out, "Numero Uno?"

Paul tapped her shoulder. "Lily, darling, I need to tell you what happened to Victor."

But Lily refused to respond. Though Paul only mentioned an accident, she had an ominous feeling Victor hadn't survived his crash.

"Colonel, what time's the funeral on Saturday?"

Danny's question made Lily's fear turn to anguish.

Lily managed to hold back tears until her room was darkened for sleep. A night-light cast eerie shadows on the walls, and she imagined Victor lurking in them. How could he be dead?

She'd begged Paul not to encourage Victor's military pilot dreams. Something bad could happen to him, she'd warned. Her son's husky laugh, soft brown eyes, and hearty hugs haunted Lily as she beat with clenched fists at a pillow soaked with tears.

By the time a morning sun rose in the frigid January air outside Lily's memory unit window, she felt numb and depleted of emotion. Her body was stiff as though injected with starch. Her eyelids seemed frozen. She wondered if this was what it felt like to be dead.

Staring into an electric-blue sky, the disjointed face of that man whose name Lily had been struggling to remember floated past like pieces of a jigsaw puzzle. She could hear his hearty chuckle, see his captivating eyes, smell his exotic aftershave. Frantic to connect his face with a name, Lily heard the last thing he had said to her: "If you ever need me, just call."

Tom Eberson. Suddenly, his name shot through Lily's fractured memory. Tom could help her.

When Nancy brought a breakfast tray and cracked, "Another gourmet feast from the local restaurant," Lily pushed it away.

"I'm not hungry, Nancy, and need to ask a favor."

Nancy's wide smile disappeared as she ran a thick

hand across her pink nurse's uniform and eyed Lily. "Have you been crying?"

Lily shrugged thin shoulders beneath a navy bed jacket and stared at her hands, which fluttered like wings of a wounded bird. "I want you to call someone."

"Why not let your husband do that?"

"No!" Lily's voice shook. "It's a secret."

"Mrs. Lily, I can't get involved with secrets. Maybe you should calm down and rest a bit." Nancy stroked Lily's hand as if comforting an infant.

Lily threw back her bedspread. "You think I'm crazy just like Paul does. My memory may come and go. But I'm going to show you all I'm sane."

"Mrs. Lily, we're going to get you dressed now. Today we're going to work on your memory box, remembering the old days when your sons were little tykes." Nancy retrieved a photo from a cardboard box and held it up. "See? There you are with Victor."

Lily stared at a beautiful young woman posed on a boat dock, curvaceous in a red swimsuit, gazing with adoration at the little boy in her lap. She looked blankly at Nancy. "Who's that?"

As Nancy helped Lily bathe and put on a gray pantsuit, Lily kept repeating, "No memory box." She was still saying it, rocking in her chair, when Paul arrived with Danny.

After Paul finished his clean-up, he started toward the door. "Danny, I'll get us coffee."

The minute Paul left, Lily ceased chanting and rocking. "Danny, can I use your phone?"

"What's up, Mom?" Danny stopped texting. "Got a secret lover?"

"You've always been my jokester and best keeper of secrets." Lily flashed a conspiratorial smile at her son. "Your father is not to know about this, okay?"

Danny, who had a red bandana wrapped around his forehead, grinned. "Any chance to fake out the Colonel works for me." He handed Lily his phone. "I'll leave so I won't be tempted to spill your secret." He winked at her. "I'm not sold on the idea you belong here. You seem pretty sharp to me."

Locating Tom Eberson in Directory Assistance was easy. Before Lily's mind had become cluttered with cobwebs, she'd secretly kept track of Tom's whereabouts. Even though she and Paul agreed to delete Tom from their lives, Lily had refused to erase her treasured memories.

On the answering machine, Tom's deep, alluring voice made Lily's heart do a flip-flop.

She left a message: "Tom, it's Lily. You said to call if I needed you. Please come right away. My son Victor has died and I need your help to leave here." She provided the address.

In case Paul returned before Danny, Lily put the phone on the rocking chair. She realized her heart, though leaden with grief about Victor, was beating erratically at the thought of seeing Tom. What would she say when he arrived? And what would Paul do?

As questions tumbled through Lily's mind, she

decided it'd been a mistake to phone Tom. She was about to call again to say, "Don't come, Tom," when Danny and Paul returned. She closed her eyes.

"I've never seen anyone sleep as much as your mother," Lily heard Paul say.

"Colonel, if I were stuck in this joint, I'd sleep all the time, too."

"The funeral is day after tomorrow." Paul paced. "I have to tell her about Victor today."

"Mom understands more than you think, Colonel."

"TGIF. Time to wake up, Mrs. Lily." Nancy laughed. "You're like Rip Van Winkle, asleep since yesterday afternoon."

"What day is it?"

"Friday. Your son Nick is coming today."

If today was Friday, tomorrow was Victor's funeral. Lily had decided overnight to try and delay the service until Tom came and heard what she had to say. Surely they wouldn't have the funeral without her. So she'd pretend to sleep until tomorrow to allow Tom time to arrive.

"I'm so sleepy, Nancy." Lily executed a dramatic yawn.

"I declare, Mrs. Lily, you've turned that ole forty winks into four hundred. You need to get dressed. Maybe go to a group art class? Too much sleeping's bad."

Lily was tempted to shout, "Don't be like Paul and tell me what to do." But she did not want to alienate Nancy, the only one who made this place bearable.

After getting dressed Lily sat in her rocker and drifted into dreams. Her dreams had always been as disorganized as Lily's daily life. Now, they were chaotic. Yet, their featured players remained the same—Victor, Paul, and Tom.

In this dream, Paul blew Lily a kiss as he boarded a plane while Tom descended in a parachute. Tom handed Lily a gift-wrapped box. But Paul appeared and snatched it. Then Lily faced a row of Air Force officers, including Paul and Tom and Victor, arranged like a police lineup. "Choose only one," a voice ordered as Victor waved from his plane cockpit before his arms and head detached and hurtled toward Lily.

Lily had no idea how much time had passed—a half-hour, a half-day, even two days—when she heard Nick's gentle voice. She pictured her skinny, pale son. During his last visit Nick wore horn-rimmed glasses and a platinum crew cut. Each time he came, his hair was a different style and color. But hairdressers had to experiment, Lily supposed.

After Nick had professed his preference for men over women, Lily tried to shield him from Paul's disdain. Nevertheless the chill between father and son had remained. The only person who'd been able to smooth the awkwardness was Danny, who was joking now to defuse the tension. "Nickster, the Colonel and moi—"

Lily heard the door open and Paul erupt: "Tom Eberson, what the hell are you doing here?"

"Well, that's some greeting after all these years." Tom's tone was neutral. "Lily still looks like an angel."

Lily fought a temptation to open her eyes to see Tom's rugged jaw and generous mouth.

Paul's voice was brusque. "Danny and Nick, this is Brigadier General Tom Eberson, an acquaintance from military days."

As hellos ensued, Lily stole a peek. Luckily Tom's back faced her. After a quick glance at Tom's broad shoulders and still-slender waist, Lily shut her eyes.

"Boys, could you leave Tom and me alone for a while?" Paul asked.

"Oops. Looks like the Colonel wants to have words with the General," Danny cracked before they left.

Tom began to march back and forth. "Paul, I realize what happened years ago made me the enemy. But I never meant to hurt you."

"Didn't mean to hurt me?" Paul's voice quivered with outrage. "Of course not. You've always commandeered whatever or whoever you wanted even if it belonged to someone else. Tom, you have no idea how much harm you've done."

"I already apologized. I'm sorry about your loss. Victor, I mean."

"How did you find out about that?"

"Lily called and asked me to come."

"You not only hurt people but you lie," Paul yelled. "Lily couldn't have called. She has no phone."

"If you don't believe me, Paul, ask your wife."

As a hush fell over the room, Lily felt herself in the spotlight. It made her recall other long-past spotlight moments: standing in a high school gym where bright lights illuminated her and other prom court members; sitting in a chair as Paul bent on one knee to say she was the gem who'd make his life complete; wearing a corsage and watching Victor deliver a commencement speech which cited the influence of his mother.

Lily's moments in the spotlight had faded as time passed and etched lines on her face while sabotaging her memory. Now, she craved one final starring role.

She stood and flung an arm toward the men who stared at her. "Tom has come to take me out of this awful place. But first I need to tell him about Victor." Mentioning her son caused Lily to break down in tears.

Paul moved to Lily's side. "Please calm down, sweetheart."

Lily frowned at her husband. "Stop telling me what to do."

Paul leaned close to Lily. "Please don't say what I think you're about to. It doesn't matter now because Victor is gone. I need to tell you about that."

"Paul, I already know. And I'm sick of everyone treating me like I'm a deaf moron." Lily gestured toward Tom. "He deserves to be told the truth about Victor, and you're not going to stop me."

Tom's green eyes flitted between Lily and Paul. "Look,

I'd best be going. I didn't come here to stir up something, only to support you in the loss of your son."

"Your son, Tom." Lily's voice quavered. "Victor was yours."

Three years after they'd wed, Lily sat on their bed with her back to Paul. Her slim shoulders sagged and her white-blond hair hung over her lowered face. She'd clutched her stomach and whispered, "This is Tom's baby not yours, Paul. I'm so sorry. Tom must never find out."

A devastated Paul had requested a transfer from the Air Force base where he and Tom were stationed. After they'd moved Lily and Paul tiptoed around her betrayal as though treading on land mines. They had visited a therapist where Lily wept while Paul grimaced.

As her pregnancy progressed, Lily had showered attention on Paul as if being a model wife might make him forgive her. She had berated herself, too, watching circles beneath her husband's eyes deepen and his sturdy frame shrink to skeletal proportions.

Finally, they'd come to an uneasy truce to salvage their marriage: Paul would forgive Lily; she would not misbehave again; he would raise Victor as his own son; neither would ever mention Tom Eberson.

Though Paul never admitted to Lily that it was hard to pretend Victor was his own son, she'd suspected so. Yet, Victor had been such a lovable, affectionate child that everyone, including Paul, gravitated to him. And when

Victor had excelled at whatever he tried, Paul was quick to boast of his accomplishments.

Despite her guilt, Lily had missed Tom—his muscular arms around her, his constant compliments, his impetuous nature. Her life became dull without their stealthy get-togethers and physical passion. Lily, who'd loved to jot down romance novel plots, saw Tom as the dashing type who broke women's hearts. He reminded her of quicksilver, and his unpredictability made her heart race.

Yet, Lily had been certain that Tom, unlike Paul, would make a fickle husband. When she'd first met Paul at an ice cream social, Lily was on the rebound from a daredevil boyfriend. Paul's steady, kind temperament had seemed a calm harbor in the turbulent waves of Lily's life. She'd welcomed the adoring security Paul offered.

Despite the infidelity episode, Lily and Paul had woven a harmonious marital tapestry over the years. Lily had sought the excitement she craved in other ways—at military parties where she flitted about like a stunning butterfly gathering nectar, at her artist's easel spreading vivid oil paint with abandon, in her daydreams fantasizing about romance.

Occasionally people who knew Lily had commented on her evident pell-mell gusto for life. That had prompted Lily to quote her mother's advice: "Go out and grab what you want from life. Don't wait for it to grab you."

On Saturday morning, Lily was wheeled into a small church adjacent to the memory facility. It was a tranquil setting of stained-glass windows, a metal cross, and a simple oak altar. Red carpet covered the stretch of floor from the vestibule to the altar railing. At the front, a flag-draped casket was positioned with tall baskets of white flowers on either side. Sweet scents of calla lilies, mums, roses, and peonies permeated the air.

In the past Lily might have raved about the gorgeous flowers. Today she seemed not to notice them or her husband and sons at the private funeral.

Nancy, who pushed the wheelchair down the aisle to join the men, had dressed Lily in black. Someone had teased Lily's hair into a bouffant pageboy and swirled rouge circles on skin as white as bleached cotton. Her eyes were wide open as if frightened.

The chapel door opened again and Tom stepped in. Medals dangled from his blue military uniform like ornaments on a Christmas tree. He moved with precise steps down the aisle as if at a military drill, glaring at Paul.

Danny stared at Tom. "What's General Eberson doing here, Colonel?"

"Isn't this just for family?" asked Nick.

Tom stopped in front of Lily's wheelchair, his face contorted with rage. "Lily, couldn't you have had the decency to let me know about Victor? I thought you had more respect for me."

Paul moved to Lily's side. "Tom, you should have

thought about respect years ago before Victor was born. Now is hardly the time or place to delve into that."

Tom squared his shoulders. "Don't try to shut me down, Paul, like you and Lily have done all these years by keeping me in the dark."

Lily's glance skittered from her husband to her sons and past her lover before settling on the casket. "Oh, my men. I have all of you here together, except Numero Uno."

Paul touched Lily's fingers, trying to quiet their incessant taps on the metal wheelchair arms. "Don't say something you'll regret, Lily."

"You know what I regret, Paul?" Lily stopped tapping and pointed at him. "Not telling Tom or our boys the truth. Maybe years of living a lie are what destroyed my brain."

Lily's eyes filled with tears. "Do you have any idea what it's like to not know what day it is, not recognize people, feel everything slipping away and you can't do anything about it?"

Tom's expression softened. "We're all sorry for you, Lily. But you and Paul did a terrible thing not to tell me about Victor."

Danny stared at Tom. "I always knew something was different about Mom's Numero Uno. He looked exactly like Tom."

A side door of the chapel opened and a robed minister walked in and shook everyone's hands. "Are we ready to start the service?"

"Forgive!" Lily's fingers yanked at her teased hair

until it stood out from her head in spiky pieces. "Tom's baby! Numero Uno!"

"Pastor, please excuse my wife." Paul motioned to Nancy to take Lily away. "This is too much for her. She's probably having some of her hallucinations."

Tom looked from Lily to the casket. "All of this feels like one giant hallucination. But Lily belongs here for the funeral. Don't send her away, Paul."

Turning to face the casket, Tom saluted it. His voice broke. "Now, let's bury our son. We can do this together."

Lily looked at Tom, then Paul and her sons, with no flicker of recognition.

SUNSHINE

Ethel Jones, in her fluorescent, lime-green crossing guard uniform, was an immutable sight at the busy corner of Third and Ash Streets. She waved and flashed engaging smiles at motorists while tending children, who filled a void for someone denied motherhood. For over a decade she'd managed to never show favoritism among the kids.

Until Gabby Simmons came into her life.

After Gabby had entered Winston Elementary last fall as a first-grader, Ethel watched hired help bring the child to school. One nanny in a turban and blue jeans. Another speaking broken English. They did not appear to mistreat Gabby. So Ethel couldn't fault them for dereliction of duty. Still, Ethel was convinced she could do a better job and was concocting a daring plan to rescue Gabby when school ended in a few weeks.

Integral to Ethel's plan was transforming her late husband's one-room office into a hideaway for her and Gabby.

To keep her project top-secret, she was doing all the work herself to make the drab office a wonderland of pink, the little girl's favorite color. A ruffled pink bedspread. Filmy pink curtains. A dressing table with a pink skirt. She'd spent an entire weekend hanging wallpaper with fat, pink roses, cursing strips that kept ending up crooked.

Sam's accounting office, in a rundown building bordering the inner city, was forty minutes across town from Ethel's bungalow. The littered neighborhood had deteriorated since Sam chose it. Youth roamed aimlessly or loitered in alleys. Businesses and residents barely survived. But the office had a sink, refrigerator, and bathroom so it was livable.

Ethel's main worry about being discovered with her captive child was Reggie Sims, who sold used bric-a-brac in a first-floor storefront across the hall. Reggie was skinny and hunched with beady eyes and filthy fingernails.

Recently, as Ethel left the office, Reggie shoved his way past her and peeked inside. "Well, well, pretty fancy. What's going on in there?"

Ethel felt nauseous inhaling Reggie's rank odor. "None of your business."

He pointed a crooked finger at Ethel. "Reggie's gonna keep an eye on you, Missy. You're up to something." He disappeared into his store.

Ethel's hand trembled as she locked the door. Now, she'd have to factor Reggie into her rescue plan.

Twice a day Ethel made the fifteen-minute walk to

her crossing corner from home on a street lined with stately oaks. She prided herself on never having missed a day of work despite pain from severe arthritis that wracked her five-foot, two-inch frame.

Until a year ago she'd looked forward to finding Sam waiting for her after work. He'd have a cup of tea brewing each afternoon when Ethel returned. Now Max, their Labrador, was the only one at home since Sam's fatal heart attack.

Without Sam, Ethel dreaded the nightly silences lurking throughout her bungalow. When the grandfather clock struck or Max barked, sounds seemed to careen from floor-to-ceiling. Constant quiet sent Ethel's imagination reeling.

Stealthy intruders might be lurking outdoors. Burglars could be hiding in the basement.

Insomnia plagued Ethel for the first time.

One late March evening, Ethel's plan to rescue Gabby began percolating. She'd sat brooding about her future in her kitchen with its pink, lace-trimmed curtains. Pink made her think of dear, giggly Gabby. Spring snow had just fallen and that morning the child's round face had peered out at Ethel from the fur-trimmed hood of her pink snowsuit.

"Mrs. Jones, I made a snowman." Gabby grinned, producing a dimple on each chubby cheek. "He has a pink scarf."

Ethel had an overwhelming urge to embrace this delectable little girl despite the nanny's presence. Instead, she'd asked, "Gabby, do you have a pink bedspread and curtains in your bedroom?"

"Yes. Mommy calls me The Pink Princess."

Envisioning Gabby's sweet face snuggled in bed beneath a pink blanket, Ethel wondered if dressing in that color head-to-toe herself would make Gabby like her more.

The issue of negligent nannies was only one of the reasons Ethel had decided Gabby must be rescued. The child's family situation, which Ethel had investigated, was another.

One day Gabby had shown up holding the hand of a skinny teenager in holey jeans and a skimpy crop top, who was texting on a phone.

Ethel despised the sight of cell phones on which nearly all the nannies and parents seemed to be chatting or checking messages while ignoring the kids. Ethel owned no such phone and did not intend to join those she considered fanatics, who were fixated on these devices.

Ethel approached Gabby and the teenager, whose gaze was glued to her phone. "Are you Gabby's new nanny?" Ethel winked at Gabby, who smiled and revealed two missing front teeth.

"I'm her sister, Nan." The girl chewed gum and towered over Ethel in platform shoes.

"Do you have brothers or other sisters?"

"Nope."

"Why don't your parents ever bring Gabby to school?"

"My mom, you mean? She travels a lot for work." Nan shook her thick, black ponytail and frowned. "What's with all these questions?"

Ethel speculated: So here was an absentee mother with two daughters who'd, no doubt, hardly notice if one of them was gone. "Gabby, come along." Ethel took the child's hand. "I'll help you across the street."

As they walked, Ethel put her mouth, thick with red lipstick, close to Gabby's ear. "Honey, would you like to come live with me for a while?"

The child looked confused and wary. She searched Ethel's face with vivid blue eyes. "I need to go now. Bye, Mrs. Jones."

After work that afternoon, in Ethel's miniscule front hall, Max yipped and gyrated. He followed her to the kitchen where she chose a blue teacup, from a collection that crowded kitchen shelves, before brewing the lemon tea Sam used to fix. She'd been trying to diet and shave pounds off her pudgy frame but gave in to the temptation of one chocolate chip cookie.

Max, drooling on the patterned kitchen linoleum, looked mournfully at his jar of dog biscuit treats until Ethel tossed him one. Then he crouched at her feet, gnawing his snack.

"Maxie, you're a good listener. But I wish you could talk and give me advice." Ethel patted Max's shiny, black coat. "I've talked to you before about this adorable child,

Gabby, coming to live with us. I need to figure out whether to rescue her at school or at her house. Once it starts to get dark tonight, you and I are going to check out where Gabby lives."

After a supper of scrambled eggs and rye toast, Ethel headed out to her aged, black Honda. She doubted that Gabby's sister, who might recognize her, would be outdoors. But just in case, Ethel was wearing a dark stocking cap over her dyed hair and all-black clothes. Wintry weather had vanished, and it had been atypically hot all day. Sundown had not brought coolness and Ethel was perspiring in her black outfit.

"You're probably hot, too," she told Max, who got in the car and sat upright in the passenger seat. She was thankful that he was also black. As they drove off, Ethel imagined the two of them as spies off on a secret night mission.

As Ethel reached the 900 block of Elm Street, she inched the car along, looking for house number 917, then parked across the street. The Simmons home was a replica of Elm Street's lineup of modest ranch houses with a brick exterior, concrete walk to a small square porch, and an attached one-car garage. The yard looked untended with a few straggly evergreen bushes.

Based on Gabby's fashion parade of countless pink outfits, Ethel had expected the family to live in a grander house. Yet, if Gabby's single mother was supporting two daughters plus a nanny, Ethel reasoned that a lavish house was probably not affordable.

A sleek, white Cadillac with out-of-state license plates was parked out front. As Ethel stared at the house, a man came out holding the hand of a woman whose face was a grown-up carbon copy of Gabby. She had the same thick, dark curls, pert nose, and engaging smile. Slim in tight jeans and a leather jacket, she resembled a teenager more than a mother of two.

Ethel muttered to Max, "Well, well, that has to be Gabby's mother. She can't manage to bring her child to school but finds time to run around with some man. All the more reason I should rescue Gabby."

Max moaned in response to Ethel's strident tone.

After numerous nights of surveilling Gabby's house and watching her mother depart, Ethel concluded that Ms. Simmons did not travel as much as Nan had indicated. She'd also begun to suspect that the man with the out-of-state license plates might live at 917 Elm Street since he was always there.

One night as she and Max sat across the street, a different man sprinted up the sidewalk, rang the bell, and was greeted with a hug by Gabby's mother. "Don't tell me Gabby's mom is not only neglectful but promiscuous," Ethel muttered. "Good thing I'm going to do something about this disgusting situation. She'd have been called a loose woman when I was young."

In order to execute her rescue plan seamlessly, Ethel had laid out the timeline and details on yellow legal pads.

Since Ethel planned to stay home all day with Gabby, the rescue had to occur as the school year and her crossing duty ended in May. But Ethel was still fretting about exactly how to take possession of the child. She scrawled various scenarios on pads labeled "Rescue Day" before settling on this approach:

After the nanny left Gabby at the crossing corner the last morning of school, Ethel would keep the child at her side until she'd finished with all the other kids. Then she'd conjure some excuse to take Gabby to the Honda parked nearby and whisk her away. By the time school authorities phoned Gabby's home about her absence, Ethel and the little girl would be ensconced in the pink bedroom.

Whenever the opportunity had arisen, Ethel gathered facts about Gabby's preferences. She wanted to make sure everything Gabby desired would be on hand.

"Sweetie, what's your favorite cereal?" was one question for Gabby.

"Froot Loops."

Ethel disapproved of such a sugary cereal but bought several boxes anyway.

"Honey, do you have a favorite doll?"

"Samantha, my American Girl doll. I love her."

Ethel knew this line of historical dolls was quite expensive. But soon Samantha was tucked beneath the pink blanket of Gabby's bed.

The answer to every question Ethel asked Gabby resulted in more shopping. Gradually Sam's office got jammed with tea party plates and cups, skirts and sweaters in a tiny closet, storybooks about princesses—nearly all of it pink.

The most prized item Ethel had added to the room was an enlarged photo of Gabby.

She'd toted her camera to school one sunny day and taken the shot after Gabby's nanny left. The little girl, in a pink jumper and hair bow, had smiled and waved at Ethel in the color photograph that now starred on a bookshelf.

One evening as Ethel fussed around the pink bedroom, she composed a mental letter to be mailed to Gabby's mother the morning of Rescue Day. It would say:

"Dear Ms. Simmons,

You are lucky to have your beautiful Gabby. But a dear child like her deserves special care, which you, her nannies, and her sister don't provide. She needs someone who can love her to death."

Ethel paused. "To death" was not appropriate. She'd substitute "like a devoted mother."

As Ethel composed the letter in her mind, she toyed with the notion of listing all the justifications behind her rescue. But opting for brevity, she concluded:

"So I have rescued Gabby and will care for her until you either decide to be a dedicated mother or at least hire a nanny who speaks English and isn't always on the phone.

Yours truly, Ethel Jones."

In the last few days before the end of school, Ethel rehearsed each rescue detail as though she were producing a stage play. She decorated Gabby's bedroom with fresh pink carnations, bought sugar cookies for a tea party, and laid out pajamas decorated with pink fairies. She even instructed Max to behave himself in case Gabby was afraid of dogs.

The night before Rescue Day, Ethel began to worry and consulted Max. "What will we do if Gabby is scared to stay with us?" She stroked his big head. "What if her mother or Reggie calls the police?"

Max sprawled in a spread-eagle pose on the floor as Ethel rambled on.

"But the police would understand that a neglected child needs rescuing, wouldn't they?" Ethel looked at Max who'd fallen asleep. "I just know they'll agree with what I've done."

After Ethel crawled into bed in her paisley pajamas, policemen, nannies, and Sam paraded through her dreams. A procession of Gabby's nannies appeared and scowled at Ethel as a stern-faced cop stepped up to say, "Mrs. Jones, we need to have a talk with you." Then Sam patted Ethel's cheek and said, "Honey, I know you've always wanted a little girl to replace the one we lost. But this is the wrong way to get her."

Ethel's dream spun into her recurrent nightmare of the evening Sam had rushed her to the hospital as grinding pain shot through her swollen stomach. As Sam's car raced along, Ethel had reasoned that her baby was far enough along to survive.

After Ethel had emerged from the anesthetic, her doctor delivered a heartbreaking verdict.

Their baby daughter had died.

Afterward, Ethel found herself obsessed with babies. She had wandered up to strangers' baby buggies and peeked inside, or watched Gerber baby ads on TV and wept. She and Sam had no interest in adoption and tried to create another child. But as the years passed, no little girl or boy had come to join their family.

By dawn Ethel had a crushing headache and her heart rate was churning. Putting on the crossing uniform, she vibrated with nerves. She tried to down the usual oatmeal but her stomach felt too queasy. She picked up Max's leash. "Maxie, it's Rescue Day. You're coming to school with me. Today you'll finally meet Gabby."

Stopping at a postal box, Ethel clutched her handwritten letter addressed to Ms. Simmons. She hesitated, knowing the launch of Rescue Day was going to change her life. But she was not about to toss out her dream of mothering Gabby. She opened the mail slot.

When Ethel arrived at her crossing corner, the kids were as ecstatic about school's final day as adults might be celebrating TGIF. It was a glorious May morning with puffy clouds in a cerulean sky. Ethel tried to act normal, not nervous, as youngsters cavorted about her. Every few minutes she glanced down the street, hoping to spot Gabby and her nanny.

As the corner emptied, after the last kids were crossed, Gabby had not appeared. Ethel stood rooted in place, unable to process her devastation at this setback. It had never occurred to her that Gabby could foil a plan that seemed foolproof.

Trudging toward her Honda, Ethel heard Max barking through his open car window down the street. How could she explain to him that the rescue plan she'd described, the piles of toys he'd watched her accumulate, the photo of Gabby she'd shown him—all of her exacting preparations had been derailed and her chance to rescue Gabby thwarted?

In the car, Max was so happy to see Ethel that he licked away the tears on her face. As she continued to cry, he barked and growled as if to make her stop. Once he'd given up, Max lay his head in Ethel's lap.

Ethel patted him. "We have to go by Gabby's house and see what's going on, Maxie."

Over the front door at 917 Elm Street hung a "JUST MARRIED" banner. In the yard fat balloons attached to sticks proclaimed "CONGRATULATIONS."

Ethel was so unnerved by this discovery that she overshot the curb while parking. "Poor Gabby. Her mom will be even less interested in her if there's a new husband."

As Ethel sat brooding about the sabotage of Rescue Day, the nanny came out with Gabby. The child was a fluffy vision in pink—an ankle-length dress trimmed with ruffles, matching ribbons woven in her hair, and a small bouquet of pink roses.

Behind the nanny and Gabby came Nan in a filmy red dress with her hair in a sleek chignon. Then came Ms. Simmons, parading as though she were already walking down a church aisle. She wore a fitted cream gown that hugged her curvy figure, and held her long skirt up off the ground. She walked gingerly in satin high heels.

All of the wedding party laughed in the bright morning sunshine as they strutted down the sidewalk like models in a couture show.

Watching Gabby, Ethel felt her dream of motherhood fade like a momentary rainbow might. Visions of Gabby in her pink bedroom—delighting in a tea party, playing with her doll, wrestling with Max—crashed like broken crystal into scattered fragments.

For a moment Ethel felt detached from it all as though it were someone else who had decorated a child's room, plotted a daring rescue, and mailed an ominous letter.

The thought of that letter brought her back to reality. Ethel visualized it traveling from the postal box into a mailman's hand and up the sidewalk at 917 Elm Street. Ethel imagined Ms. Simmons looking puzzled at the unfamiliar handwriting on an envelope with no return address. She envisioned Ms. Simmons's pretty face changing from bewilderment to fury as she read the short letter. Ethel did not want to speculate about what Ms. Simmons was apt to do.

Then there was creepy Reggie. Ethel could imagine him blaring to all the neighbors, and maybe even a policeman who patrolled the area, that something suspicious was going on in an all-pink room across the hall.

Ethel felt flushed and short of breath as though she'd just completed a marathon. With a trembling hand, she started the Honda. "Maxie, there will be another Rescue Day. Very soon. But right now, you and I have to get lost for a while."

Mort and Milly

Opening her front door, Lana Clark called, "Mort and Milly, I'm home!" When the parrots failed to warble their usual "Lana home," she figured they must be hiding. The babysitter who tended them often left their cage door open so the pair could roam.

Lana's high heels clicked room-to-room over mahogany floors and plush carpet as she wooed her African Grey parrots. "Mortie, babe? Milly, sweetie?" She looked in their favorite hideouts—beneath her canopy bed, behind silk curtains, in the Jacuzzi tub. Playful searching turned to palpable fear as Lana ran out of hiding places.

Mort and Milly were gone.

Lana, an advertising executive, liked to tell people that the parrots provided humor and equilibrium in her life with their silly antics and crazy word combinations. What she didn't confess was they had become substitutes for the children she'd never have and an unfaithful ex-husband. The birds gave her a reason to go home after work to the elegant twelfth-floor Chicago condo that had felt empty and cold since Keith Clark left.

Divorce had shaken Lana, shattering her ability to trust. "How could I have misjudged Keith so completely?" she was still asking her psychiatrist two years after their nasty split.

Lana had met Keith on the rebound from her broken engagement to David Wills, a charming banker. David had ended it abruptly, with vague comments about wanting a different lifestyle than Lana. Three months later he'd wed someone else, which generated Lana's trust issues.

During her divorce, Lana had worked on an ad campaign featuring a talking parrot. She'd realized such companions wouldn't criticize or abandon her as David and Keith had. Now, she relied on Mort and Milly for affection. They warmed her heart with "Hi, Lana" or "Love you."

Panic engulfed Lana now as she considered that someone might have stolen her parrots. Each bird had cost fifteen hundred dollars. Maybe somebody had taken them to be sold. Or might it be revenge of some sort? Whoever took them had access to her condo and knew when she'd be away. That included Penny James, her bird babysitter, though Lana considered her trustworthy.

Lana felt her usual composure evaporate. She wondered whether this was how it felt to be stalked.

Down in the sleek, marble-floored lobby accented with potted plants, Lana rushed up to the doorman. "Cecil, you know my precious parrots, my babies . . ." To her embarrassment, Lana broke into tears.

"Now, Ms. Clark, calm down." He scanned Lana's slim figure in a stylish black pantsuit. "Your babysitter bird lady Penny took them out this morning, said they were visiting the zoo."

"Did Penny bring them back?"

"I didn't see them. I was gone for a dental appointment so maybe they came home then."

"Did anyone else who visits me come today?"

He looked at black mascara streaks around her wet eyes. "Your sis, Deb, came by. So did Gary, your boyfriend. Said he'd left something at your place and needed it right away. I knew you wouldn't mind since he's a regular visitor."

"Gary Fillmore is a friend, not boyfriend, Cecil." Lana did mind that Gary, who was pursuing her in earnest, felt he could enter her condo without asking permission. Admittedly she was attracted to classy, cultured Gary. Yet, Lana was hardly ready to rush into another relationship, no matter how delectable the man might be. She was furious at herself for giving him a condo key in a weak moment.

Upstairs, Lana checked each room to make sure nothing besides the parrots was missing. Then she phoned Penny and left a message telling the bird sitter what happened and asking her to call back right away.

After slipping her long legs into designer jeans, Lana freshened her makeup in the newly remodeled master bathroom. It made her think of Hank Souter, foreman for the project that transformed a dull beige space to an airy wonder of granite counters and creamy walls. During the renovation, he'd had a key and returned it. She supposed he could have replicated it first. *Lana, that's crazy. Be rational,* she told herself. *Why on earth would Hank steal birds? Get a grip.*

Lana stared at herself in the bathroom mirror. She saw a forty-two-year-old face that was more striking than beautiful—angular with high cheekbones and framed with jet-black hair cut bluntly below her ears. Her dark eyes looked fearful, as they had during her divorce. Lana asked her mirror reflection, *Why is someone trying to punish me, and who is it?*

It was August and Chicagoans thronged city streets as if to drink in balmy breezes soon to be replaced by frigid winds. Lana lived downtown near Michigan Avenue, known as the Magnificent Mile, which had an upscale pet shop where she'd purchased Mort and Milly.

Inside Palmer's Pets, where hounds howled and parakeets tweeted, a young man with one earring was pinch-hitting for the owner. He listened to Lana's story, then said, "Those African Greys are real smart, five-year-old level. They know how to escape and get back home, even if it means flying a ways. I'd put their cage outside with food and see what happens."

"Please tell the owner, who sold me Mort and Milly, they're missing," Lana said.

Walking home, Lana answered her phone and heard Gary's smooth voice. The handsome lawyer and the birds had not hit it off. The first time he came over, Mort and Milly objected by acting obnoxious—screeching and fighting. They'd reacted the same around Keith.

Both men had uttered some version of "Why the hell would anybody want a couple of squawking birds?"

Despite Gary's negative feelings about Mort and Milly, Lana was hopeful he'd warm up to them eventually. She liked his company and would hate to give up the Chicago Symphony and Lyric Opera outings he provided.

"Gary, I guess you stopped by my condo today," Lana said on the phone. She pictured the rimless eyeglasses that made him look intellectual and the curly hair that invited a caress. "Why couldn't it wait till I was home?"

After Gary explained he'd accidentally left a legal file behind on his last visit and ducked in to retrieve it, Lana asked, "Were the birds there?"

"No. What's going on?"

Her voice cracked. "I guess it will make you happy. Mort and Milly have disappeared."

"Don't be silly, Lana. Of course it doesn't make me happy if it's hurting you. I may not like birds but I'd never do anything to them. It's you I care about."

"I have to go now. Next time we're together, I want my condo key back."

"Why?"

"I need to retrieve all the keys I've given out. That's all."

Turning off Michigan Avenue onto a leafy side street, Lana dialed Keith. Waiting for him to answer, she told herself to remain calm with a man she'd once thought irreplaceable but now found impossible. "Keith, I called because Mort and Milly are missing. I wonder—"

"I suppose you're accusing me of having something to do with it. I'm not the villain you're convinced I am. Instead, maybe you should ask yourself why all you think about are those damn birds."

Keith's angry retort and stinging criticism reminded Lana how she'd wanted to hide when he had such tantrums. She envisioned his hands clenching in rage and his finely pored skin turning red. Lana tried not to raise her voice: "I thought you might have an idea how to find Mort and Milly. Forget it. By the way, did you find my condo key you said was lost? I want it back."

Keith's fury prompted Lana to think about her psychiatric sessions with Doctor Len Babcock. Notes she'd jotted after each session revealed her pattern of behavioral issues—high control need, lack of trust, and emotional barricades.

Sometimes after a session, she asked herself: *Was I always like that or did the divorce change me?* The answer continued to elude her.

Tuesday morning Lana was due to make an important PowerPoint presentation at her downtown office in a majestic high-rise with sweeping views of Lake Michigan and Navy Pier.

She'd hardly slept, and a haggard face greeted her in the mirror. She avoided the kitchen where the parrots usually engaged in animated chatter or swooped about as she had morning coffee.

Downstairs, she got Cecil's permission and put the birdcage outside near the door.

Walking to work, Lana told herself, *Mort and Milly will come back. They wouldn't leave me.*

Twenty minutes into a presentation to clients in a darkened conference room, Lana saw "URGENT. CALL ME." flash on her phone screen. Then Cecil's name popped up. "Excuse me for the interruption but I need to return a call," she said, racing out of the room.

"Your parrots showed up back in their cage while I was away on my coffee break," Cecil reported. "I put them in your condo."

After rushing through the rest of her presentation, Lana headed home. In the lobby, Cecil was conferring with a man whose poodle was barking. Waiting, Lana watched Cecil in his impeccable suit and bow tie. She found it odd that he had either been absent or not noticed when the birds were transported through the lobby. She knew Cecil's salary was low, and he had to support several kids. Surely he wasn't a thief or in cahoots with someone who was.

When he finished, Lana asked, "Cecil, did whoever substituted while you were on break see who put Mort and Milly in their cage?"

Cecil lowered his voice. "You know Willy, the sub? Nice but not too sharp. Claimed he never noticed."

It was unlike Cecil to criticize others, thought Lana, heading upstairs.

Entering her front hall, she expected Mort and Milly to squawk, "Lana home." She rushed into the kitchen to find an empty birdcage. Someone had been here again and taken them away after Cecil returned the parrots to her condo.

"Somebody's playing games with me, trying to make me lose my mind," Lana said out loud. "It's making me paranoid, suspecting people closest to me."

Lana checked her phone messages. Penny, the bird sitter, had not called back which was unlike her.

Then she phoned her sister, Deb, and left a message to return the call. The siblings, two years apart in age, were so disparate that it seemed like they might have grown up in different families. Lana was willowy and exuded femininity; Deb was stocky and a tomboy. Lana had relished school; Deb skipped college. Lana loved nature and animals; Deb disdained both, telling her sister she was "nuts to have those birds."

After their parents died in a plane crash, Lana and Deb lived with Aunt Tess. The girls were in grade school and it was clear Tess favored Deb. Lana had come to resent Deb for being treated best, and her jealousy created a chasm between the two.

Deb, who eked out a meager living cleaning houses,

answered Lana's call while vacuuming. She listened to the theft story before saying, "Birdies flew the coop?"

"They wouldn't leave voluntarily." Lana had given Deb a condo key when she and Keith moved in since her sister was the sole Chicago family member to summon for an emergency. Lana tried to sound nonjudgmental: "You dropped by the condo yesterday. Why—?"

"Yeah. Thought you might be home till Cecil said not."

"Why would I be home on Monday unless I was sick? Aren't you cleaning then?"

"Why are you being so suspicious? You're always testy about something."

Lana was about to tell Deb she needed her condo key back when the doorbell chimed. "Gotta run, Deb."

Gertie Jenkins, her stern face set in its usual frown, stood outside in the hall. Cecil had divulged that Gertie, Lana's snoopy next-door neighbor, complained often to him about the parrots' noise. "What's up with your birds?" Gertie said. "They were making a terrible racket going out yesterday."

"Did you see them leave? Penny, their sitter, took them out."

"So that's who was yelling at them to shut up. If I was a bird, I wouldn't want that woman for a sitter. Goofy to have a bird babysitter anyhow."

"Gertie, I need to go." Lana closed the door and considered whether Gertie might have lied just now. Lana recalled her condo's former owner saying she and Gertie were such good friends they'd exchanged keys. Did Gertie still have hers?

Penny worked part-time at Lincoln Park Zoo's McCormick Bird House. Lana knew Penny had taken Mort and Milly there a few times to interact with other birds in the Free Flight area. Lana decided to take the afternoon off work and see if that's where the bird sitter was.

In the lush, tropical Bird House, Lana found Penny chatting with a visitor as birds soared like colorful dancers overhead. In some ways, Lana thought Penny resembled a bird. She had a sharp beak-like nose, small eyes, and a shrill voice. Yet, she was likable and clearly loved birds.

"My cell phone broke," Penny said when asked why she didn't return Lana's call. Her thin eyebrows shot up as Lana related all the theft details. "Real weird. I brought them to the zoo yesterday, then took them home."

Lana wanted to believe Penny was innocent though she often talked about being broke. Lana theorized there was a possibility Penny had grown so fond of the parrots she wanted them for her own. Of the possible suspects, she clearly had the most opportunity. "Penny, do you have any idea who would take Mort and Milly?"

"Your ex-hubby hated those sweet birds. I'd rattle his cage, not to make a pun."

During an Uber ride home, Lana thought about contacting Keith again. She was reluctant after his last diatribe on the phone. Yet, he'd always been able to analyze a crisis more logically then she and provide expert direction.

Like Gary, Keith was a corporate lawyer. He was still angry Lana had been awarded their condo in the divorce instead of him. Keith was smart and clever, too. If he had anything to do with the theft, Lana knew he'd hire someone else to do it so no one would suspect him. So besides seeking his advice, she'd have to be cautious interrogating him.

When Keith answered his phone, Lana said, "Can we get together for a drink? Right away, at Solly's Tap near the condo."

As Keith strolled through the dimly lighted bar to Lana's table against a paneled wall, she thought of their marital history. They'd met on a blind date, two ambitious young professionals propelled into marriage by an instantaneous spark. With ample income and grandiose aspirations, they'd planned to live the high life, to travel, and have a couple of kids.

Even now Lana was not sure when their decade-long marriage began to crack. She'd wanted children more than he and was devastated to learn that would not be possible. At first he'd mourned with her until he began seeking the strokes his ego required from other women.

"Is this about the birds?" Keith put his beer glass on the table. "Lana, you look undone."

She squelched a sarcastic retort and felt the knot in her stomach that conflict with Keith inevitably caused. "I don't expect you to be sympathetic, knowing how you feel about my parrots. I'm stymied and scared. All I want is your unbiased opinion about how to proceed."

To her surprise Keith reached for her hand. "Sorry about blowing up at you on the phone. I know we went through some rough stuff, how much you wanted kids, all that. And I screwed up, literally." He wiped away a tear that slid down Lana's cheek. "But I can't take all the blame. Lana, you've changed. You used to be warm and engaging, not cold and aloof. Sometimes it seems like you're trying to drive everyone away."

Lana heard Doctor Babcock telling her: "When people have been hurt, it's easy to build emotional walls to prevent it happening again."

Keith tapped Lana's shoulder. "I'm leaving now. I meant what I said before about you caring more about those birds than people. That, I'll never understand. The only theft motives that occur to me are money or revenge. I hate to disappoint and be of no help but how one tracks parrots is beyond me." Keith flashed his deep dimples and fixed bright blue eyes on her, a look which had once enchanted her.

She studied a couple kissing at an adjacent table and wondered whether they trusted each other.

All night, Lana tossed and reviewed possible culprits. She still needed to grill Gary. Quizzing Keith, Deb, and Penny had accomplished nothing. Any one of them could be guilty. So could someone in her condo building. She'd always trusted the employees but maybe somebody besides the manager had a master key to all the units. Perhaps she should hire a detective.

Near dawn, she finally fell asleep and dreamed Mort and Milly flew onto her bed trilling "Lana home."

Wednesday morning, as Lana passed her boss's glassed cubicle, Josh Ryan called her in. "Rumor around the office is your birds were stolen. What gives?"

Lana liked Josh for his even temperament and fair treatment. She looked at a photo of his cute kids on a credenza. "I wish I knew, but frankly, I have no answers."

"Why don't you take a couple days off and deal with this?"

"But I have a presentation to—"

Josh offered his winning smile. "You won't be your old efficient self until you find your birds. Now go."

Lana's first stop was Palmer's Pets. Due to its prestigious Magnificent Mile location, the interior was deluxe—framed animal portraits on the walls, coffee and cookies on a walnut stand for customers, even a photo booth to record someone with a newly purchased pet.

Dot Palmer, the owner and a grandmotherly sort

who adored animals, was beside a rabbit cage cooing at its floppy-eared inhabitant. Dot turned to Lana. "How are Mort and Milly?"

"I asked the boy working Monday night to tell you they were gone."

Dot shook her head. "Kids nowadays are space cadets. He didn't tell me."

Lana related the jarring sequence of events. "Honestly, Dot, I'm spooked."

"This may be just a coincidence, but the same kid said a guy came in last night asking if we knew anyone who bought African Grey parrots. The kid said no and told him we only bought ours from Africa. I didn't think anything about it, not knowing your sweeties were gone."

Lana's heart lurched. "Did he say what the guy looked like?"

"Just good-looking, didn't seem like a geeky bird type. Whatever that means."

Keith? Gary? Both fit that description. Lana knew her former husband would never visit a pet store. Gary might dislike birds but hardly needed money from selling parrots. Yet, could Gary possibly think that if the birds were gone, she'd have more time for him?

"Oh, and your bird lady Penny keeps dropping by to visit Hector, the only African Grey parrot we have left. She goes on and on about wanting to buy him but doesn't have the bucks."

As Lana headed home, mulling over the theft suspects,

she stopped at her favorite deli for a tuna sandwich. After two bites she threw the rest away, too distressed to be hungry. She decided to call Gary, request a meeting, and try to find out if he'd visited Palmer's Pets.

Approaching her front door, Lana noticed something taped to it. The crudely-printed note, on letter-size paper, read:

"$1,000 FOR THE BIRDS OR YOU'LL NEVER SEE THEM AGAIN."

Lana picked Solly's Tap again to meet Gary. He was already there, resembling a Brooks Brothers ad in his tailored navy suit and striped tie. He stood, kissed Lana's cheek, and eyed deep circles beneath her eyes. "I've missed you."

"We're not here to discuss our relationship." Lana fiddled with a drink coaster. "It's odd but someone at the place I bought Mort and Milly said a good-looking guy came in asking about selling parrots. Have you ever been to Palmer's Pets?"

Gary gulped scotch. "If you're accusing me of something, you've got the wrong guy. Don't you trust me?"

Lana fingered her pearl necklace. "I'm sorry. This is just so painful, and I'm hardly a detective. Do you handle extortion cases?"

"No, my law firm doesn't handle cases that small, and I can't moonlight."

"So I'm on my own. Remember I want my condo key back?"

"I forgot to bring it. Next time." He looked morose. "I hope this drama is over soon because I miss the Lana I used to know."

"What do you mean, Gary?"

"You seem so angry, even hostile. You're shutting me out and treating me like I've done something terrible to you." Gary left without kissing Lana goodbye.

That night Lana lay trying to concentrate on a plot to ensnare the extortionist. But Gary's claim of her treating him badly, the rift between her and Deb, and Keith's accusations kept coursing through her mind. Reviewing their comments, Lana realized that each of them had characterized her as a wretch.

By dawn Thursday Lana had vowed to make amends for her shabby treatment of people. She'd also come up with a simple plan to confront the parrot thief.

Mid-morning she contacted Penny, Deb, Keith, Gary, Gertie, and Cecil to say she was leaving town for a few days in case they needed to reach her. She positioned the ransom note demanding money on her kitchen table beside her own note, dated Thursday. It said:

"Mort and Milly must be back here on Friday by noon before $1000 will be paid. I will be out of town but someone will check to make sure they're both here. The money will be on the table Saturday morning after the birds have gone somewhere safe."

She departed with an overnight bag for a hotel. She'd arranged with Beth, her administrative assistant, to check on Friday whether Mort and Milly had been returned. Afterward, a courier would transport the parrots to Palmer's Pets for boarding.

Near noon Friday, Lana was pacing her office waiting to hear from Beth, who had gone to the condo. Finally, the phone rang.

"Your birds are here," Beth reported. "They look fine."

"Hallelujah! The courier should be there soon."

Early Saturday morning Lana entered her condo, put the envelope on her kitchen table, and moved coats to make room to hide in the front hall closet. She'd just finished when footsteps sounded in the hall. She ducked into the closet and fought shortness of breath from nerves as someone came in.

It was pitch-black in the closet and Lana began to feel claustrophobic. She waited as footsteps entered the kitchen. Minutes ticked by but no one left. Lana was entertaining the awful prospect of being in the closet for a while when the person headed for the front door.

Lana threw open the closet door. "Deb!" she yelled.

"You're the thief? How the hell could you put me and the birds through this?"

Deb, the envelope clutched in her hand, whirled around. "I was never going to get rid of Mort and Milly or harm them. That was just a threat. I need money, and you have so much."

Lana trembled and looked at her sister with eyes blurred by tears. "Do you know how it feels to find out your sister is spying on you, keeping track of your comings and goings, sneaking into your condo, and stealing? Of everyone, I least suspected you."

Deb locked eyes with Lana. "Do you know how it feels when a sister you adore rejects you?"

"What did you think stealing Mort and Milly would accomplish?"

Deb shuffled in tattered tennis shoes. "I hoped if you lost the things you love most, you might realize how selfish you've become, acting like you're better than everyone else. I miss the sister you used to be."

"Everybody's accusing me . . ." Lana took a deep breath. "There I go again, having a pity party. I vowed last night not to do that anymore." She frowned at Deb. "So you tried to make your point by stealing my parrots. How did you get them past Cecil in the lobby?"

"I used the back deliveries-only door."

Why didn't I think of that? Memory took Lana back to Deb's resourcefulness when, even as a kid, she was adept at hatching solutions to tricky problems. She might have eschewed education but Deb had highly developed street smarts.

"Deb, it's going to take me a while to get beyond this stunt," Lana said. "But I—"

"Here." Deb stepped forward and offered the envelope of cash.

Lana pushed it back, then extended her arms for an embrace. "Keep the money. Even though I'm really ticked off at you, I intend to work hard to improve our relationship."

"Look, Lana, I understand that with the birds back you're feeling forgiving and generous." Deb ran fingers through cropped brown hair. "But I can't switch and be your lovey-dovey sister all of a sudden just because—"

"I give you a thousand bucks, forgive your inexcusable theft, and offer to make up. What more do you want?"

"See? There you go again. It's all about Lana, always has been." Deb pulled out Lana's condo key and placed it with the money on the table. "You think an apology gives you the right to erase all your past behavior and have control over everything. You'll never have any decent relationships, Lana, until they're balanced fifty-fifty." Deb rushed out and slammed the door.

"Ungrateful as usual," muttered Lana. "At least Mort and Milly appreciate me."

That afternoon Lana heard the parrots squawk as the courier brought them back. "Lana home," they repeated. Then Mort chanted "Go away."

"Smart Mortie learned new words." Lana opened the cage and one bird perched on each of her shoulders. She nuzzled them. "Welcome home."

By six o'clock Lana was waiting for Gary to pick her up for their dinner date at Spiaggia, a romantic second-floor restaurant on Michigan Avenue. She'd dressed to look glamorous with a sequined black top and leather skirt, and makeup emphasizing her eyes and lips.

Gary eyed her but didn't offer his usual kiss. "You look nice."

"So do you." Lana felt unsettled by his aloof greeting.

"Go away," Mort squawked from the kitchen.

Gary said, "So the birds are back. I trust I'm no longer suspected of having inquired about selling them."

Lana glanced at her watch. "We should go."

"Go away," Milly warbled.

At dinner Lana struggled to sustain conversation as Gary seemed unusually quiet.

He waited until coffee to say, "I considered cancelling tonight. I haven't really gotten over you mistrusting me."

Lana reached for his hand. "Let's forget about that."

"No. If we can't trust each other, how can we go forward?" Gary handed Lana his condo key. "Whether we have a future is up to you."

Sunday was a classic August beauty with cloudless skies and brilliant sunshine. Lana hoped a long walk might chase away her gloom and set off for the lakefront. Streets were crowded with runners, dog walkers, bikes, and baby strollers. Near the lake she saw Keith approaching in sweats and dark glasses. He held hands with a statuesque blonde but stopped laughing when he spotted Lana. It was too late to detour.

As they arrived, he said, "Lana, small world. This is Suzette."

"Are you THAT Lana?" Suzette had a syrupy Southern drawl.

"I'm in a hurry." Lana jogged away.

Lana's disastrous Saturday with Gary, and Sunday with Keith, clouded the start of a jam-packed week—a client report to her boss, an evening art show, a psychiatric session.

Near week's end she was sleep-deprived and grouchy. Neither Gary nor Deb had contacted her, and she had no energy to call them. Even the antics of Mort and Milly failed to uplift her.

On Friday Penny called to say she was sick. She'd send her daughter, Jill, to take the birds to the zoo.

That afternoon Lana was about to leave her office for a TGIF drink with a colleague when Penny phoned. She was sobbing so hard Lana could barely understand her.

Jill had transported the birds in their portable cage but, accidentally, hadn't fully latched its door. When Jill opened the car, one parrot flew out. The other followed.

"Oh my God, they're gone again!" Lana shrieked, realizing this disappearance was different. Mort and Milly were completely free. They could go wherever they pleased.

As Lana raced home to put the empty birdcage outside again, she agonized about the dangers facing parrots who'd never spent time outdoors. They could be attacked by larger birds, struck by a bus or car, even starve. It was too dark outdoors to launch a search.　Lana lay awake all night imagining the worst.

At dawn Saturday Lana began roaming her neighborhood calling "Mort? Milly?" Near noon, taking a break in a park, she heard Mort's distinctive squawk. Lana looked up and saw him perched on a power line. "Mortie, come to Lana," she called, wondering where Milly was.

"Go away!" Mort flew off.

Lana ran in the direction he'd gone, gazing up in case Mort might reappear. When she heard him squawk overhead at a busy intersection, Lana stepped into the street still looking up at the sky. Honking cars swerved to avoid her. But one hit Lana broadside.

Lana awoke in the hospital's ICU with myriad tubes connected to her body. All she could recall was being thrown against concrete and an ambulance siren. Then she remembered Mort—his silhouette against the sky, his "go away" squawk, his disappearance. She ached at the thought of losing him and Milly.

Lana slipped into a disturbing dream. Mort and Milly swooped by but vanished as David and Keith appeared. Each of them itemized Lana's selfishness and shortcomings. Deb came after the men. She yelled, "Lana, you almost died because of those parrots. Why can't you care about the rest of us as much as you do them?"

Opening her eyes, Lana saw Deb standing beside her bed. Lana was confused—had Deb scolded her in the dream or had she been talking in the hospital room?

Deb reached for Lana's hand and squeezed it.

Lana wanted to talk but felt so weak. All she could manage was "try to change . . . if I make it through this."

A Butterfly Connection

Mindy flopped onto a tattered sofa in her drab apartment and clicked on a late-night *Moments in Time* soap opera rerun to repress details of her sordid evening. Hopelessness stalked her as it did every night. At twenty-two, the optimism that had brought her to Hollywood was evaporating like dew on a sun-scorched flower.

She'd gone to countless acting auditions, hell-bent on replicating the girl who sang and danced her way to fame in Mindy's favorite movie, *La La Land*.

But her big break had not come.

Sometimes she dreamed about home in Indiana—tasting her mom's crispy fried chicken, feeling warmth from a crackling fireplace, stroking the silky fur of her cat, Angel.

Mindy had fled home heartbroken, determined to erase memories of Jeff Robins, whose betrayal with her best friend had destroyed her trust in men.

On *Moments in Time*, Carolyn, a statuesque lawyer,

who wore provocative outfits and conducted extramarital affairs, flashed a smile at Bruce, who was married to someone else. She flipped shoulder-length blond hair and extended her right index finger. Enameled on her nail was a dazzling metallic silver, turquoise, and hot-pink butterfly. Glitter on its wings made the butterfly seem bathed in a spotlight.

"Wow!" Mindy imagined the butterfly taking flight as Carolyn's hand moved.

Mindy's dad had taken her as a child to a conservatory where neon blue and tangerine orange butterflies alighted on her shoulders. An English teacher, he had quoted Charles Dickens: "'I only ask to be free. The butterflies are free.'"

Bruce whispered in Carolyn's ear and ran a finger down her bare back. His boldness catapulted Mindy to furtive scenes of her own in bedrooms and cars, where men who'd hired her as an escort explored her body but never murmured endearments.

At first Mindy had done part-time jobs—waitress, sales clerk, even dog sitter—but was usually broke. Until recently when a fellow waitress proposed an escort service: "This woman, Sylvia, only accepts wealthy guys as clients and pays really well. No kink or danger and totally discreet."

Mindy's eyes widened. "Is it more than being an escort?"

"Sometimes. The money for that is amazing."

Mindy cringed. Accompanying someone to a party or dinner might be harmless. But she'd sworn off intimacy after Jeff. Yet, approaching escort work like an acting role would be great practice. She could playact TV's Carolyn, staying emotionally uninvolved with men and letting them slip through her life as if they were hired actors. Besides, the pay was too alluring to pass up.

She executed her transformation to Carolyn by dressing her willowy physique in a sexy, sophisticated style with dark eye shadow, pink rouge, and red-hot lips. She splurged on a replica of Carolyn's fingernail butterfly. After a hairdresser trimmed her shiny black hair to the length of Carolyn's, Mindy practiced before a mirror to flip it like she did. Every night Mindy studied Carolyn on TV and taught herself to laugh, flirt, smile, and walk like the soap star.

For her introductory interview with Sylvia, the madam, Mindy wore a miniskirt and leather boots she thought Carolyn would choose for such a meeting.

The madam conducted business from her paneled study in a rambling Los Angeles house where several bedrooms were designated for assignations. Sylvia, whose once-stunning beauty had faded like an aged photograph, eyed Mindy.

"Pardon my staring but you remind me of someone. The way you flip your hair. Your smoky dark eyes." She raised razor-thin eyebrows that matched her dyed brown pageboy. "Maybe someone on TV but I'm not sure who." After a stream of instructions, Sylvia concluded, "My girls use fake first names."

"I'll be Carolyn."

Back home, where a Murphy bed folded out of the wall, Mindy grabbed a beer and turned up the TV volume of *Moments in Time* to drown out the street noises.

A sinister-looking man tiptoed into a shadowy library and whispered to his companion, "The club safe is supposed to be behind the left bookcase."

The library door flew open and Bruce strolled in. His pause in the inky library gave the thieves time to hide beneath a conference table.

Mindy laughed, waiting for Bruce to detect the cowering robbers. Then she gasped as the door opened again and Carolyn's white teeth flashed in the dim light.

Bruce raced to embrace Carolyn, led her to the conference table, laid her across its top, and kissed her. Carolyn's finger butterfly glittered like a beacon in the dark room.

Following a TV ad, Carolyn was heading with her husband, Charlie, to the exit. He said, "You seem upset, Carolyn. All I want is for you to be happy."

"Oh, Charlie my love," Carolyn cooed in the voice Mindy had been practicing.

"Shit!" Mindy hit the remote control off button. "She's got a husband who adores her and an unfaithful jerk who does, too. It's not fair."

The parade of clients Mindy escorted had little in

common except affluence, a penchant for secrecy, and at least one major personality flaw. She documented them in a leather-bound notebook captioned: "Carolyn's Clients." After each outing Mindy jotted down a man's characteristics as though she were a psychiatrist analyzing him as a patient.

Matthew, a state senator, was so tightly wound that relaxation was a foreign concept. Frederick, a gruff German, could be counted on to make lewd comments. Rex spouted so many obscenities about his wife that Mindy concluded she must be detestable.

Of them all, Mindy found Kenny the most troubling. Raw psychological wounds from Vietnam made him explode with comments like: "People should be crucified for treating us vets like garbage when we came home from 'Nam."

When Kevin Flood, who'd directed two Hollywood musicals, appeared on Mindy's escort roster, she was ecstatic. Maybe this was her lucky break, that entrée onto a movie set.

At a cocktail party the next evening, she strove for Carolyn's nonchalance as Kevin slurped one martini after another. By night's end she dreaded a second date with the portly and boastful director. But she was determined to land an audition for his next musical.

After several dates Mindy had grown no fonder

of Kevin and was grateful he'd not insisted on physical intimacy. Sloppy kisses on her cheek were the extent of his affection.

Each time she saw Kevin, Mindy brought up her desire for an audition. The night he finally said, "Okay, you can audition tomorrow for my next movie," Mindy threw her arms around his rigid body but got no hug in return.

The audition was for an ingénue role. Interpreting that as a teenager, Mindy pulled her thick hair into a ponytail and put on minimal makeup. Aiming for a 1950s look, she put on a white cotton blouse with a Peter Pan collar, a navy skirt, and black ballet-style flats.

In the sparsely-furnished audition room, Kevin sat at a table with several others. No one smiled or said hello. Kevin handed Mindy several pages of dialogue. "Three minutes to look it over. Then start."

Mindy's heart began to thump as she scanned it and realized she shouldn't have dressed like a teenager. As she read aloud, her voice shook. Several pairs of eyes dissected her, which made her voice quiver more.

"Enough!" Kevin shouted before Mindy finished the first page. "Whoever said you were a good actress was wrong. And those clothes you have on are ridiculous."

Mindy lowered her head and considered challenging Kevin. But tears were threatening and she was not about to cry in front of him.

Kevin followed her to the front door and yelled, "Best

stick to escorting, not acting. And you need to wise up. Even the most naïve escort should be able to see that some guys prefer men to women. Guys like me."

"I can't do this anymore." Mindy sat before Sylvia's desk the day after her disastrous audition and scanned a vase of cascading purple orchids. After lying awake all night torturing herself about the audition and Kevin's accusations, Mindy had decided she'd return to waiting tables or selling clothes to fund her auditions.

"What brought this on?" Sylvia's imperious voice rang out. "Last time we talked, you were all excited about Kevin Flood."

"He turned out to be a jerk. I'm sick of guys like him."

Sylvia tapped a manicured nail on her desktop. "Kevin's off the list then. But I'm going to make it up to you. His name is William. He's CEO of L.A. Reserve Bank and wants absolute privacy with no local outings. Don't bring up his work and meet him at bedroom three. Four o'clock tomorrow."

"But I don't want another—"

"I have an appointment in two minutes. We'll talk more next week."

Mindy couldn't muster enthusiasm for William. She was furious at herself for not standing up to Kevin, then letting Sylvia sabotage her decision to quit. Carolyn would never have let either happen.

Vowing to never see this William again after one meeting, Mindy put on old black slacks, a plain cream blouse, and minimal makeup and headed to Sylvia's bedroom. Its black-and-red décor made Mindy feel sleazy. The bed sheets were blood-red and the shag carpet black. Sylvia insisted these hues promoted ardor.

When William knocked, Mindy opened the door and said, "Hi. I'm Carolyn."

At over six feet and in his thirties with curly dark hair, William wore glasses and a businessman's stereotypical navy blazer and tan pants. Yet, when he smiled, Mindy's heart lurched. His engaging smile mirrored Jeff's and spread across his mouth like thick syrup oozing over pancakes.

William sat in a wingback chair across from Mindy. "My wife is institutionalized and bottom line, I have no one to talk to." As William described his wife's mental illness and its impact, Mindy tried to find fault with him. Perhaps beneath his likable façade was an egotistical, un-trustworthy CEO.

As the hour wound down, William said with that smile, "I'd like to see you again."

"That's not possible."

"Did I say something to upset you?"

"I'm just not into men right now. I—"

William's eyes widened. "Sylvia should have told me you're a lesb—"

"No, it's not that! I just can't see you. That's all."

At first, Mindy was exultant about leaving the escort world. Then she learned that her former employers no longer needed her. Isolated in her apartment searching want ads, the walls seemed to close in on her. Blaring car horns on the street made her want to scream. Some days she didn't even bother to change out of her bathrobe, and she fretted daily about her dwindling savings.

She dreaded bedtime when her dreams, which used to star Jeff, featured William with his captivating smile. At the sight of him in each dream, Mindy panicked and tried to run away. Yet, her feet were trapped in quicksand. Her auditions were not going well either. Someone was always prettier, danced better, or had the best singing voice. Her only friends were random street people—the guy at a newsstand on her corner, a clerk at the grocery store, the cranky landlady.

On *Moments in Time*, Carolyn had been conniving to snare Felix as her latest extramarital prize. As Mindy watched the TV star's finger butterfly flit by, she lamented that her own fingernail ornament had brought only bad luck.

One night Carolyn said, "Felix, as a banker you can help me—"

Mindy jumped up from the couch and yelled at the TV. "What the hell is wrong with me? I had my own banker and blew it." Carolyn, she knew, would use someone like

William for her own benefit but hold him at arm's length in case she felt attracted to him.

"Has William called?" Mindy asked Sylvia on the phone the next morning. "He's been asking for me? Okay, I'll be there tomorrow afternoon if you promise he'll be my only client right now."

The next day, Mindy immersed herself mentally in being Carolyn. She chose a metallic, scoop-neck top to coordinate with the shiny silver on her fingernail butterfly, and wore thick, black eyeliner and extra mascara.

At Sylvia's bedroom mirror, Mindy primped and practiced Carolyn's facial expressions until four o'clock. When William failed to appear, she began to pace. "I should have known he's no different than Jeff," she muttered. "Inconsiderate. All about him." As she was turning off the lights to leave, he rushed in.

"Crises at the bank, Carolyn. No time to call you. Sorry." He flashed his smile and buried his head on Mindy's shoulder like a child seeking forgiveness.

Mindy pulled away, flipped her hair, and did a Carolyn-style shrug.

William became increasingly comfortable with Mindy. He revealed: "I feel trapped in my marriage. I've been considering divorce."

Once, as he reflected how his wife's illness had decimated their happy marriage, tears welled in his eyes.

William's evident pain touched Mindy. Yet, she'd steeled herself against an emotional response, patting his hand. "I'm so sorry."

Each time William left Mindy, he hugged her. Despite resisting, she'd begun to long for the feel of his smooth cheek against hers and the scent of his woodsy aftershave, which reminded her of her father. When he kissed her on the forehead one day, Mindy felt a rush of affection that she tried to quash by focusing on Carolyn.

On *Moments in Time* that evening, the soap opera star had been toying with Felix like a mouse taunting a cat. In the latest episode, Felix raced through a room of travel posters to a woman's desk. "Got the tickets, Julie?"

Outside the travel agency, Felix phoned Carolyn. "Baby, our trip is on. Jamaica here we come!"

Carolyn wailed to Felix, "Oh my love, I have something upsetting to tell you."

"TO BE CONTNUED" flashed across the screen.

Mindy slapped a hand on the sofa. Why did the soaps always have to leave viewers hanging in suspense? What if Carolyn was going to say her husband was terminally ill or their son had died? She imagined all sorts of horrendous possibilities.

The following Monday Mindy listened to William complain again about his wife.

During a long and boring weekend, she'd fought imaginary vignettes of outings with him. A beach stroll where they held hands. A terrace where they toasted one another at twilight. Not since Jeff had she so craved someone while struggling not to.

Listening to him now, Mindy heard the loneliness in his voice. She wondered whether her own misery was evident when she talked. "You'll figure a way out of this, William," she reassured while pondering whether her own fate was that of a wretched, frigid spinster.

Heading home, she replaced thoughts of William with speculation about whether Carolyn would invent an excuse tonight and tell Felix she couldn't go to Jamaica. Before *Moments in Time*, she changed into jeans and fixed popcorn, anxious to learn the verdict.

Carolyn, eyeing her finger butterfly, said into a phone: "Felix, I don't think we should see each other anymore."

"I knew it!" Mindy said.

Felix's face was a mélange of grief and shock. "Carolyn, you can't do this. Please!"

Carolyn looked unfazed by Felix's laments. Her expression was one of smug triumph as though she'd never cared for him at all.

The next time Mindy met William, he arrived acting nervous with a bottle of wine.

After they'd each had two glasses, he proposed a toast: "Even though we've, well, we've only talked, I wonder if you'd like to go with me to my place in Jamaica."

"Jamaica?" Mindy's gaze roamed floral wallpaper above the bed. Alcohol scrambled her thoughts. A trip sounded so romantic but Carolyn had decided against Jamaica. Mindy heard herself say, "I don't think we should see each other anymore, Felix."

"Felix? Who in the hell is that?" William's usually-even voice was tinged with hurt. "Why shouldn't we see each other?"

Mindy blinked, sending tears down her cheeks. Staring at the red bedspread, she took a sip of wine, then launched into the story of Jeff Robins, not looking at William until she'd finished.

William said nothing at first. Then he moved to Mindy and caressed her cheek. "Now I understand. It's about trust." He put on his coat and headed toward the door. "I hope you know you can trust me. Please decide to come to Jamaica."

"I need to think about it, William. I'll let you know next time we're together."

As Mindy headed home, images of William's face alternated with that of Carolyn. For weeks, Mindy had wanted only to be reincarnated as her soap star idol. Using men. Discarding men. Locking her heart against men.

Now, Mindy's resolve to be Carolyn was crumbling with the realization she'd just inflicted cold cruelty on William.

Yet, Mindy wondered: If she had already turned her back on being herself but no longer wanted to be Carolyn, who was she going to be?

By midnight Mindy was dreaming of Jamaica. Carolyn and Felix were perched on bar stools in a thatched-roof hut as Mindy strolled in with William. Mindy's turquoise strapless sarong, chosen to set off her tan, complemented her colorful finger butterfly. As Mindy introduced herself, she said, "What a coincidence that we're both named Carolyn."

In her dream William blurted, "Mindy, you're so beautiful. Like a butterfly."

A tide of warmth enveloped Mindy. For the first time since high school when she'd tap-danced across a stage in *Singin' In The Rain,* she felt euphoric. "William, I'm sorry. I want to go—"

Mindy awoke, threw on her shabby chenille robe, and fixed a cup of tea. By dawn she was counting the hours until she could phone Sylvia and request a meeting with William as soon as possible. To calm her nerves, she turned on the radio as a distraction.

An announcer was summarizing the latest news.

"The CEO of L.A. Reserve Bank has been killed in a robbery. William—"

Mindy screamed, shoved her right index finger in her mouth, and began to chew off the butterfly.

The Jimbo Plan

Some nights Lori Wilson felt like a newscaster delivering progress updates to her mother, Rhonda, and her mom's sister, Nadine Perkins.

In Nadine's cluttered kitchen, Lori flashed a satisfied smile at the pair. "It's taken three months but Jim genuinely believes I'm the daughter he lost track of as a baby thirty years ago. I'm on the verge of getting some of the money Mom needs for her back surgery."

Nadine tied on a flowered apron. "I love Jim Connor but I hate being his housekeeper. I deserve a fancier life, like the one I had before my jerk of a husband took off." Nadine looked at Rhonda's fragile frame. "Lori, don't forget the reason you're chasing Jim's fortune is your mom. The doctor said unless Rhonda has spinal fusion surgery, she could end up in a wheelchair."

Lori nibbled a fingernail. "I have a major competitor in Ginger, Jim's fiancée. Nadine, you said she's after his money, too."

Nadine nodded. "In Ginger's desk, I found the code

to access messages on the private phone line she set up after moving in with Jim. Ginger's up to no good. Today this guy calls and says: 'Honey, I missed your sassy buns on the treadmill this morning. I got new info about our Jimbo plan.'"

"Jimbo? Could that be Jim?"

Nadine, who'd kept house twenty-five years at Jim's palatial Chicago Tudor, winced. "Might be. I figure there's one reason a babe half Jim's age intends to be Mrs. Connor. Greed. Maybe this phone guy is helping Ginger plot how to get her hands on Jim's money."

A troubled look clouded Lori's sweet face. "I feel guilty lying to Jim. But he lies, too, introducing me to Ginger as his goddaughter. He told Ginger he didn't have kids. So he's afraid she'll leave if he admits having a child. Ginger resents any woman involved with Jim and doesn't want me at their wedding."

Three months earlier in March, when Nadine proposed her scheme to extract money from Jim, Lori resisted. She loved her mother and wanted her to get well despite a rocky childhood with Rhonda and her string of boyfriends. Yet, Lori found the prospect of masquerading as the daughter of a stranger scary. What if Jim, a supposedly savvy attorney, suspected fraud? What if he asked details about her mother?

Nadine had countered all Lori's fears, including her

biggest one—that Jim might insist on a DNA paternity test. "Jim has confided in me ever since his wife, Laura, died two years ago. That's how I found out the girlfriend he had before he met Laura gave birth to a baby girl, then vanished. So a snoop like me would know about a DNA test."

Nadine's money scheme involved Lori writing Jim a letter. It said Lori's mother had identified Jim before her recent death. Since Lori had just moved to Chicago, could they meet?

After Jim had agreed to a get-together, Lori agonized over what to wear. She longed to look sensational. Yet, if she dressed too well, Jim wouldn't think she needed money. Her paltry salary as a secretary hardly financed designer clothing anyway. So she'd visited a consignment shop and picked out a simple and flattering black A-line dress.

By the time Lori had arrived at Jim's office in a Michigan Avenue high-rise, she was so nervous that sweat dotted her forehead despite Chicago's frosty spring weather. Though Nadine had raved about Jim's good looks, Lori was surprised how youthful he was—lanky and trim with an infectious smile.

For lunch they had gone to a stylish French bistro on the ground floor of a different high-rise. Lori had never experienced such elegance—white orchids on side tables, a decorative fountain in the room's center, leather banquettes along the walls. The menu of unfamiliar items like quiche, escargots, and croque monsieur sandwiches was so baffling that Lori asked Jim to order for her.

As if Jim sensed Lori's nerves, he put her at ease by confessing he was also nervous.

Before their food arrived, he'd looked her over. "We have the same coloring. Dark eyes. Black hair, or mine was till it turned gray. No doubt in my mind we're related."

In their hour together, Lori had developed a headache from concentrating on role-playing Jim's daughter and calling him Dad. She'd waited for him to ask some version of "How can I be sure you're really my daughter?"

Instead, he had raved about Lori's beauty and his happiness she'd found him. He'd furnished few personal details other than being widowed and engaged to Ginger.

"I'd love to meet Ginger," Lori had said several times. She was puzzled that Jim seemed reluctant to set up a meeting. It made her wonder if he might be embarrassed about the age difference between him and Ginger.

When Jim finally agreed to introduce Lori to Ginger, he chose Bottoms Up coffee shop near his office as the site. The upscale setting, with original oil paintings on paneled walls, was teeming with handsome young professionals.

Ginger arrived from fitness class in leggings, halter top, and pink tennis shoes. Her bouncy brown ponytail evoked an ingenue who might have been Jim's daughter. "Jimbo!" she exclaimed, then kissed him. She beamed at Lori. "What a treasure, my soon-to-be hubby."

Compared to flashy Ginger and the shop's clientele,

Lori felt painfully plain in a consignment navy pantsuit. After Ginger got a latte, Lori thought of Nadine's reference to a Jimbo plan. She was tempted to blurt, "What do you have planned for Jimbo?" Instead, she listened to Ginger prattle before saying, "You must be so excited about your wedding. What's the date, Ginger?"

"Soon. But it will be so small I'm afraid you can't attend."

"Not too small to exclude my goddaughter." Insistence threaded Jim's voice.

Ginger blew a kiss at Jim. "I'm planning it, remember, sweetie?"

After a half-hour of awkward small talk, Ginger stood. "Gotta run. Here goes the bride to shop for a gown. See you after the wedding, Lori."

Jim watched Ginger prance away. "I'm a lucky man, don't you think?"

Lori studied Jim's distinguished face. All her life she'd longed for a father and fantasized about marrying a kind, handsome man like Jim. Someone wealthy would be even better. Then she could wear expensive clothes and live in luxury, not crammed into Rhonda's tacky apartment. Her greatest fear was ending up as a miserable spinster like Nadine or sick and alone like her mother. Why should some ditz like Ginger get to live the dream Lori coveted?

Twice a week Lori met Jim for lunch at Angelo's in

downtown Chicago. Jim had long frequented the casual Italian spot with red walls and candles stuck in Chianti bottles. Each visit he introduced Lori to tantalizing dishes with exotic names. Carbonara. Fettuccine Alfredo. Cannelloni. She'd come to love the delicious aromas swirling through Angelo's. Sometimes Jim offered her a sample of his cream sauce or a bite of his beloved osso bucco. She had never considered that food could be so sensual.

Yet, even at Alfredo's, Jim continued the charade of introducing Lori to waiters as his goddaughter.

Finally, Lori balked. "Why do you lie about me to Ginger and everyone else? My mom was a liar. I don't want my dad to be one, too."

Jim fingered a worn menu. "I promise to tell Ginger about you once we're married."

"She made it clear I'm not welcome at your wedding. Why?"

Jim studied his water glass, ignoring the question.

Angelo's was on a street of boutiques and ethnic restaurants that drew throngs of pedestrians. It was a balmy June day and passers-by were reveling in sunshine. As Lori glanced out the window, she gasped. Across the street Ginger walked arm-in-arm with a muscular man in athletic sweats.

Jim stared at Lori. "Are you all right, Lori?"

"Um, sure, Dad. Just watching the well-dressed people out there and thinking how nice it'd be to afford their lifestyle." She was tempted to tell Jim to look out the window.

"If it's money you need—"

"Dad, I'd never expect you to pay my way."

After ordering lasagna Jim said, "You have every right to be upset about my not being truthful with Ginger about you."

"There's still time to tell her before the wedding. Speaking of that, why do you keep postponing it?"

"Ginger and I have financial matters to settle."

"Whenever the wedding is, don't you want your daughter there?" Lori offered a saccharine smile.

"Look, honey, some troubling personal things have me preoccupied. It was a complete shock when you crashed into my life. You and I are still getting to know each other. My dear, late wife is the only one I ever confided in."

Lori reached across the red checkered tablecloth to stroke Jim's hand. The warmth of his skin made her tingle. She had to remind herself of Nadine's plan. "Dad, you can trust me."

Jim hesitated. "Okay, here goes. Ginger doesn't want to sign a prenup. My lawyer friend is convinced she's after my money. I disagree. But he insisted on a clever plan to test her and I reluctantly agreed. My main preoccupation right now, though, is health."

Lori searched Jim's pale face. "Are you okay?"

"I'm having medical tests. Please keep that a secret."

Between bites of luscious tiramisu at Angelo's the

following week, Jim said, "Ginger's insisting on a lavish African honeymoon. My girl loves to spend dough. Good thing I've got plenty."

Lori raised her thick eyebrows. "You're so lucky. I've never had any money."

Jim eyed Lori before pulling out a checkbook and scribbling a thousand-dollar check. "Sweetheart, please take this for starters. I'm so happy to have you in my life."

"Dad, thanks." Conflicting emotions clogged Lori's thoughts as she stood, walked around the table, kissed Jim's cheek, and inhaled the scent of his aftershave. She'd never dreamed getting a wad of money could be so easy.

After work Lori hurried to the bank and cashed the check. Heading home on the bus, she debated the pact with her aunt. She'd lived a pauper's existence her entire life, envying classmates with cashmere sweaters as she scraped by in bargain clothes. Even now she had to resort to wearing people's discarded consignment clothes and choose outfits that didn't look pricey so Jim would think she needed money. Now that he was giving her money, didn't she deserve to spend some of it? Nadine would never know.

Later, in Nadine's kitchen, which reeked of cooked cabbage, Lori handed her five hundred dollars and tried to look downcast. "I'd hoped for more but it's all Jim offered."

"Lori, we need a whole lot more money than that."

"Don't worry. I'll get it."

The next day on her noon hour, Lori visited a hair salon and emerged with her glossy hair styled in a sleek bob. Next, she went to a trendy boutique and chose a fashionable purple silk dress that emphasized her tall, slender frame. The fabric caressing her skin made Lori feel sexy and she couldn't wait to wear it for Jim. At work she hid the dress in her employee locker.

That night Nadine eyed Lori's hair. "Wow! That must have cost something."

"They had a drawing at work and I won a hair styling." Lori marveled at how easy it had become to lie and feel little guilt.

Nadine began pacing. "Ginger's friend called again. His name is Rick. He mentioned a life insurance policy, that Jimbo plan, and the honeymoon." She planted herself in front of Lori and Rhonda. "Sounds like Ginger and Rick have their own scheme to get Jim's money."

"Maybe this Rick is the guy I saw Ginger with downtown yesterday."

"What guy?" Nadine yelled. "Why didn't you tell us before?"

Rhonda, hunched over with back pain, looked at her sister. "Sometimes you're too damn bossy, Nadine. Maybe that's why your husband left to run an errand and never came back."

Lori glanced from her mother to her aunt and wished she could be anywhere but here.

Lori's plan crystallized one dawn as she relived another wild dream. Jim was at Lori's side as she stalked an African lion when Ginger raced toward them riding a rhino and brandishing a sword as if to destroy them. Each of Lori's dreams lately had featured the three of them with Ginger and Lori vying for Jim.

Lori realized that unless Jim's lawyer friend proved Ginger was a gold digger, Jim was too smitten with his young fiancée to give her up. Lori reasoned that if she couldn't vie for him herself, she could at least make a move to share the financial bounty Ginger was tapping.

To launch her plan, Lori invited Ginger for coffee.

At Starbucks, Lori marveled at Ginger's physique as she swaggered in wearing another form-fitting athletic ensemble.

"Hey." Ginger plopped down and fingered her blond hair.

"Hey, yourself." Lori eyed Ginger's square-cut diamond engagement ring. "You're one lucky girl to hook up with such a rich guy. Bet you're having fun with all Jim's money. If something happened to him, you'd inherit everything?"

Ginger's smile faded. "Jim keeps bugging me about this damn prenup. He refuses to set a wedding date till I sign. I don't want to."

"You know, Ginger, Jim listens to me. Why don't I try to talk him out of a prenup?"

Ginger reached for Lori's hand. "You'd do that for me?"

"It'd take lots of work so I'd expect to be richly rewarded."

Ginger's laugh was husky. "My sweetie has beaucoup dough. If you can get rid of the damn prenup, I promise to share fifty-fifty with you whatever Jim gives me going forward."

Lori strove for an innocent smile. "You and Jim seem madly in love. Do you worry about the age difference, him being so much older than you?"

"Let's just say it'll work to my advantage. Sooner, not later."

Lori thought of the Jimbo plan. "You'd never hurt Jim, would you?"

"Stay tuned, pardner." Ginger stood.

Lori knew she needed to be careful approaching Jim about the thorny prenup issue. Lately he'd been cranky at their lunches, criticizing his favorite waiter and the food, acting sullen instead of sunny.

So when she launched her anti-prenup campaign, the focal point of Lori's argument was that marriage should be based on trust. She challenged Jim to consider: If a marriage began with issues about money, wouldn't that undermine love and trust?

Yet, no matter how Lori presented her assertions, Jim countered it with insistence that money was not tied to love and trust. Money was simply a practical issue, not an emotional one, he said.

After several aborted attempts to persuade Jim, Lori was on the verge of abandoning her efforts until he was more approachable. As they consumed spaghetti and meatballs topped with Parmesan cheese at Angelo's, Jim was distracted and impatient. He was clearly in no mood for a prenup discussion. Lori eyed deep circles beneath his eyes. "Dad, are you okay?"

Jim fiddled with a fork. "It seems like all you and Ginger talk about lately is the prenup. I have more important things on my mind than money."

"You can trust me with whatever is bothering you."

Jim's eyes brimmed with tears. "I have a malignancy. My doctor is proposing surgery. Just when you came into my life and I found Ginger. What rotten timing."

As if watching a movie unspooling too fast, Lori reviewed her crash-bang history with Jim and recent alliance with Ginger. She chided herself for agreeing to Nadine's scheme. She wanted to be Ginger, the fashionable femme fatale who made Jim swoon. Instead, she'd become one of those conniving women intent on squeezing every penny out of a man. How could she have decided to deceive this precious man and compromise herself in the process?

Jim picked at his Caesar salad. "To hell with the prenup. I'm too worried to waste energy on fighting it anymore. I just don't want Ginger to find out about my cancer yet."

Nadine ran a bony finger through her gray hair

and eyed Rhonda, who was dozing after a round of pain medication. "Lori, we're running out of time to raise money for your mom's back surgery and she's in constant pain. A few hundred bucks now and then won't do it."

"Aunt Nadine, do you have any idea how hard this is? I have one fulltime job plus a second one to wrangle money from Jim."

"Don't be selfish. Can't you see how bad off your mother is?"

Lori eyed her mother, who was as fragile as a sliver of blown glass. Last night Lori had dreamed that Rhonda lay dead atop piles of dollar bills. Ginger stood beside the corpse yelling "Hey, pardner!" while Jim looked at Lori with loathing. Lori had awakened in a panic, certain Jim knew she was an imposter and Rhonda was deceased.

"Aunt Nadine, I just gave you a thousand dollars." Lori had shared half of Ginger's reward for getting rid of the prenup. She was fed up with Nadine's incessant demands for money.

"Well, step up the contributions." Nadine began to pace past Lori and Rhonda, who sat at the kitchen table. "Jim has been acting weird. He never used to snap at me. Today I saw an order form for DNA testing in his office. Did you know it can be done with a hair sample?"

Lori's heart lurched as she remembered Jim stroking her hair recently and saying it was beautiful. "I told you I was afraid Jim would want proof he's my dad."

"Lori, don't get nervous. Maybe he wants Ginger's DNA."

"That doesn't make sense." The thought crossed Lori's mind that the form could belong to Ginger, who might want to check the DNA of her fiancé and Lori. "Jim told me he prefers using checks to credit cards. Does he ever leave his checkbook behind?"

"Yeah, I've seen it in his office," Nadine replied.

"See whether Jim wrote a check for DNA testing." Lori thought of her suspicion that she was not receiving half of the money he gave Ginger, as promised. "While you're at it, Nadine, tally the amount of money Jim's given Ginger."

Nadine said, "Okay. Jim wrote a recent check I've been trying to figure out. Five thousand dollars to a R. Kravetz. Never heard of that person."

The next night Nadine handed Lori a long list of checks written to Ginger. "No wonder Jim's not giving you much money, Lori. It's all going to his greedy babe."

Overnight Lori fumed about Ginger's deception and debated how to confront her at coffee the next day. She needed to act calm, not furious.

So the next morning as Ginger charged into the coffee shop, Lori forced a smile.

"Hey, pardner, sorry I'm late. Rick and I—" A stricken look crossed Ginger's face.

"Who's Rick?"

Ginger giggled like a kid caught cheating. "Just a friend. Rick Kravetz."

Lori leaned closer. "Tell me about Rick. How you met, where he works, all that."

"I used to be a trainer at his gym. You ought to see Rick's biceps."

"A stud, huh? Say, Ginger, is Jim shutting off your money? You haven't—"

"He's turned into a real cheapskate. You get half of what Jim gives me."

"I have to tell you, Ginger, I'm disappointed with how this has turned out, all my work with the prenup for very little reward."

"Don't worry, pardner. There's a big financial payday coming. I can't tell you why or how. But it will be right after the wedding."

Lori tried to act nonchalant. "Different subject. I want to check someone's DNA. Do you know how that works?"

"Nope." Ginger examined a manicured nail. "Maybe I should check yours."

That night Nadine spooned rice onto plastic plates and said, "The DNA form's gone and Jim wrote them a check."

"Oh, my God." Lori's voice shook. "He's checking up on me and will find out I'm a phony."

Nadine patted Lori's arm. "Calm down."

Lori clutched her fork. "Ginger told me Rick Kravetz is a friend of hers from the gym."

Nadine crossed her arms across her chest. "Why would Jim pay him five thousand dollars?"

Lori pushed her untouched plate away. "If he's the guy

I saw Ginger with downtown, they're real chummy. One way to find out. I'll visit their gym before lunch with Jim tomorrow. If Ginger and Rick are in cahoots, Jim might be in danger."

The gym, which pictured a guy lifting weights on the front window, was located in a strip mall. Lori had just parked nearby when she saw Rick emerge. She was thinking what a hunk he was when Ginger raced out behind Rick and grabbed his arm. They shared a long kiss before heading to a car and speeding off.

On the way to Angelo's, Lori agonized about how to tell Jim his fiancé was a two-timer, knowing it would break his heart. Yet, she couldn't help but rejoice that a broken engagement might make her a candidate for his affection, especially after he learned she was an imposter daughter. She began to rehearse how to tell him.

After the maître d' escorted Lori to the usual table, she kept fine-tuning her spiel to Jim. When he arrived looking disheveled and wan, Lori was taken aback. He failed to deliver his usual kiss so she asked, "Dad, are you okay?"

"No." He avoided eye contact.

"Did I do something wrong?" Lori felt short of breath, dreading his answer.

"Actually, yes. Who the hell are you? Your DNA says you're not my daughter."

Lori reached for his hand, which he withdrew. "I can explain."

"I don't want explanations. You're a fraud. So is Ginger."

Lori's thoughts ricocheted. "You know about Ginger and Rick?"

"How stupid do you think I am, Lori? Or is that your real name? Rick was a paid plant to test Ginger's fidelity. So much for true love. Ginger not only cooked up this so-called Jimbo plan to bilk me but has professed her love for Rick. To hell with her. And you. This couldn't come at a worse time."

Lori sat silently until Jim, who never drank at lunch, finished a martini. Her heart pounded in concert with the animated conversations at other tables. Finally, she said quietly, "I'll make this quick." She outlined her mother's need for surgery, Nadine's money scheme, and her own ambivalence about the deception. "I'm so sorry."

Jim clenched his fists on top of the table. "None of it matters now."

"Yes, it does. I never intended to hurt you or fall in love with you." She burst into tears.

A frosty silence lingered until Jim said, "You were the one who said love should be based on trust. My law partner was right about Ginger being after my money. Just like you."

A tear slid down Lori's cheek. "Why did you say this couldn't come at a worse time?"

"My doctor has issued the proverbial advice to get my affairs in order."

"You don't mean—"

Jim threw down his napkin and stood. "Had we met under different circumstances, I might have loved you, too, Lori. But nothing can succeed on a foundation of lies."

As Lori watched Jim retreat, she repressed the urge to run after him. Her cell phone chimed and she heard Nadine yell, "Your mom fell down the stairs and injured her back. Come fast!"

About the Author

Cynthia Dennis is an award-winning journalist, and a graduate of the University of Kansas. She spent nearly two decades as a feature writer and columnist for the *Milwaukee Journal*, taught journalism while obtaining a master's degree at the University of Wisconsin-Milwaukee, and has written for magazines, radio, and television.

She is the author of *THE SUNFLOWER SINNER: An Odyssey of Politics and Passion*, published by Woodley Memorial Press.

If you've enjoyed reading *DETOURS*, please leave a review on your favorite book website. Thank you.